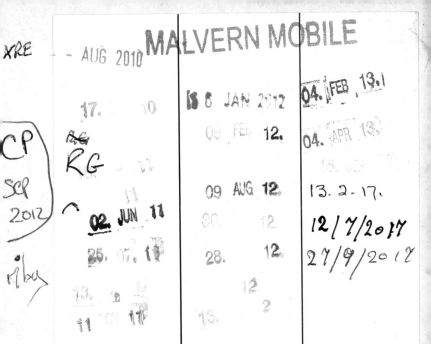

COYOTE DEADLY

When the Chulo brothers sweep into the town of Thanody, all hell breaks loose. Marshal James Tredder calls in old friend and manhunter Josh Dellin to track down the vicious killers known as the Prairie Wolves. As the West runs scarlet with blood, Josh is forced to confront a powerful landowner, protecting his guilty sons' brutal raids, whilst struggling to protect the life of a beautiful young woman who's the only witness to their foul deeds.

LANCE HOWARD

COYOTE
DEADLY

Complete and Unabridged

LINFORD
Leicester

First published in Great Britain in 2009 by
Robert Hale Limited
London

First Linford Edition
published 2010
by arrangement with
Robert Hale Limited
London

British Library CIP Data

Howard, Lance.
    Coyote deadly. - - (Linford western library)
    1. Western stories.
    2. Large type books.
    I. Title II. Series
    823.9′14–dc22

ISBN 978–1–84782–965–8

Published by
F. A. Thorpe (Publishing)
Anstey, Leicestershire

Set by Words & Graphics Ltd.
Anstey, Leicestershire
Printed and bound in Great Britain by
T. J. International Ltd., Padstow, Cornwall

This book is printed on acid-free paper

For Tannenbaum

Please visit Lance Howard on the web at: www.howardhopkins.com

1

'Looks like easy pickin's to me,' Brint Chulo said as he reined to a halt beside his older brother, Marcus, in the wide main street of Thanody.

'Sure as hell does,' Billy, the youngest of the Chulo clan, added, drawing up on Marcus's left side. 'Bet they're all nice and pure, too.'

Marcus cast his youngest brother a sideways glance and a peculiar expression drifted on to his lips. Not quite a smile, but something damn close, just a mite darker. He could almost smell the musk of innocent women in the dust-flavored air.

'You got that right, Billy boy.' Marcus leaned a forearm on the saddle horn, his scuffed-brown eyes wandering over the street's circular layout. 'Bet they'll scream even louder than them other women we visited ourselves upon.'

A laugh came from Brint, his brown eyes narrowing. 'Sure as hell hope so, but I hear tell the women here just do whatever their menfolk tell them to do and don't say a goddamn word. Hate to think they wouldn't put up some kinda fight. Never any goddamn fun when they just give in.'

'You got a black soul, Brint.' Marcus shifted in the saddle, uttered a chuckle, then went back to studying his surroundings.

Thanody, Colorado. Some sort of religious community, he'd heard tell. Peaceful. Rumor had it they abhorred violence. Well, they sure as hell were gonna get their craw jammed full of it today.

His gaze swept to the boardwalks and the numerous simple clapboard, brick and thatched-roof buildings lining the street. He noted the lack of a saloon, but this time it didn't rightly matter. He was gettin' sick to hell of bar gals and their filthy ways.

He spotted a number of women

strolling along the boardwalk, heading into stores or carrying baskets. Clothed in heavy woolen dresses and white bonnets pulled low on their foreheads, they weren't much to look at, least in the way a bar whore was, but he bet underneath it all they was hell in the sack just the same.

He noted that none of the men, all of whom wore heavy brown trousers, simple white shirts and flat hats, carried guns and that pleased him all the more. Easy pickin's, indeed.

A number of the fellas flashed them broad smiles and a tip of their hats as they sauntered by, but the women walked with their heads down, their gazes glued to the boardwalks, as if looking at strangers, especially men, was some sort of a sin. Hell, he supposed in this town it probably was.

He'd show them what true sin was like before the day was through.

'Queer as hell, ain't it?' Billy asked, puzzlement in his tone. Billy shook his head, his dull black hair straggling out

3

from beneath his battered hat, touching his shoulders.

'What is?' Marcus's gaze went back to the women.

'Way these folks jest smile like they got one foot in Heaven or some such.'

Marcus laughed, pushed up his hat and with a forearm mopped sweat from his lined brow. The mid-morning sun highlighted his mixed Mexican features and glinted from his eyes. His face might have been considered handsome had it not carried the look of a predator. Cruelty made the lines about his mouth and eyes harsher than they should have been. Someone had once told him cruelty leaked from a black soul. He reckoned that was true, and that each of the Chulo brothers had inherited that trait from their father, Miguel. Marcus couldn't damn well recollect a day that man had offered his wife a kind word or hadn't beaten the hell out of all three boys for some perceived wrong. But that upbringing had made them tough, had learned them well just what respect womenfolk deserved. Most would say the boys had taken it to entirely new levels, and those same folks would be like to admit there wasn't a damn thing anyone could do about it. The Chulo brothers were a product of their cold compassionless father and upbringing, but they held all the advantages power and money could bring, the protection.

They operated with impunity in these parts, complete freedom, and lived a life without want — but that life came with a price: boredom. And an evergrowing addiction to satisfy cravings that seemed insatiable.

That price drove the Chulo brothers to deeds few dared speak of and even fewer dared challenge.

That price had brought them to Thanody.

Billy's brown eyes were dull, the evidence of laudanum masking some of the meanness they normally showed.

'Lookee that tree yonder.' Marcus ducked his chin to a large cottonwood dead center of town. Sunlight glinted off its leaves and the warm spring breeze made a shushing sound through its branches.

'Right convenient place to hang our flags, don't you figger?' Brint said. 'Reckon it'll be a fine remembrance for the ladies of this town.'

'Menfolk, too,' Billy said, a snake of drool slithering from the corner of his mouth.

'You really oughta lay off that stuff a mite, Billy boy,' Marcus said. 'If it don't kill ya by its lonesome, it'll surely get ya killed one of these days.'

Billy laughed and stared straight ahead, at a young woman crossing the street. 'I want me that one.'

''Cause she's blonde?' Brint asked.

''Cause she's skinny. I like 'em skinny.' Billy grinned and drool dripped on to his stained bibshirt.

Marcus uttered a strained laugh. 'You never did have a lick of taste. Sure you wouldn't fancy one of the menfolk?'

'You got no call sayin' that, Marcus!'

Billy's irritation bled into his tone, but something else came with it, Marcus recognized — indignation over a fact denied but accurate.

Marcus flashed Billy a look that warned him not to push his luck, then dismounted. He guided his horse to a hitchrail and tethered the reins, while his brothers followed suit.

'Mornin' strangers,' a man said, approaching them from the boardwalk and stepping into the street. The man had a short beard without a mustache and proffered his hand. Marcus noted with disgust the flop-eating smile plastered to the fellow's face. 'Welcome to Thanody, friends.'

Marcus matched the grin. 'Welcome, indeed, but we ain't no friends of yours.' His fist lashed up, taking the man flush on the jaw. The grin vanished from the man's pulped lips. He flew backwards and down, slammed into the boardwalk, to lie half on, half off, groaning.

Marcus surveyed him. His brothers'

laughter, as well as the sight of the fallen man, brought sudden wide-eyed stares from other men walking the boardwalks. The women stopped, peering up from beneath bonnets without lifting their heads.

Marcus bent, grabbed two handfuls of the man's shirt and hauled the fellow to his feet. He pressed his face close to the other's, gaze locking on the man's watery eyes.

'Wh-why?' the man stammered through bloody lips.

''Cause I'm a downright mean sonofabitch, I s'pose.' He smiled. 'And 'cause it was just plain fun.'

'What do . . . do you want?' the man's eyes tried to focus on Marcus, but one of them seemed inclined to travel sideways in its socket.

'I hear tell you're a town without violence. I hear right?'

The man nodded. 'We are a godly town, mister. All are welcome in peace.'

'Reckon then we'll have ourselves some fun with some of your women, if

8

you got no objection?'

Stark terror and disgust washed across the man's face. But with it came the answer Marcus wanted: nobody here would lift a finger to stop them.

Marcus flung the man backward, slamming him against a support post. The impact shuddered through the man and he almost lost consciousness. His legs started to buckle. Marcus hit him again, harder, and the man's head bounced off the beam, leaving a bloody smear and strands of hair embedded into the wood.

The man slid to the ground, his body oddly ragged, his eyes remaining open, staring.

'He won't be back-talking you no more, Marcus,' Brint said, his eyes glassy with bloodlust.

'Reckon he won't at that.' Marcus's gaze traveled to the others staring at them from the boardwalks. 'Any of you got a notion to object to what's 'bout to happen here?'

Nobody made a move. Shock, horror

and fear played on their faces.

'Takin' candy from a baby,' he whispered.

Billy was already traipsing towards the slim woman he'd picked out and Brint followed only a step behind him, heading for an auburn-haired woman on the opposite boardwalk. They might be peaceful folk but they still screamed as they were dragged into buildings. Those screams didn't stop for quite a spell.

It struck Marcus as downright peculiar, the way the menfolk just watched while he and his brothers had their fill of Thanody's women. Damn peculiar. No one lifted a finger against them, no one went for a shotgun or marshal. Fact, he doubted there was even any type of law in this town. He wondered as he grabbed a dark-haired woman, heavy of breast and wide of hip, and dragged her towards a small house, how the hell a town such as this had managed to survive out here in the wilds of Colorado Territory. Seems like

10

at least Injuns would have butchered every soul in it by now. Nothing to stop them, or any hardcase for that matter, from ridin' in and takin' whatever the hell they wanted.

The only problem with the whole set-up was by the time he finished he reckoned he carried a hell of a measure of disappointment. It reminded him some of his life, how everything that came so easy wasn't worth a goddamn. The struggle was the most exciting part and though these women screamed they put up no fight when it came to surrenderin' their womanly charms.

And that was a goddamn shame.

★　★　★

Melissa Gatner stared out through the window of the small clapboard home where she lived with four other unmarried women. The old maids' house, some of them had taken to calling it, and she reckoned if she didn't find herself a husband soon that's just what she'd be. She was twenty-six after all. Practically an old maid already. She struggled to swallow the emotion balling in her throat and shook her head at her haggard reflection in the dusty glass. Her strawberry-blonde hair framed a face that would be lovely 'if she lost some of the extra weight' she was carrying, least according to the other women, and they were likely right. She was too plump of bosom and hip and round of feature to attract a hard-working Thanotite man. They liked their women sturdy and lean, sometimes even married two or three of them, though the thought of that put her in a right fretful state.

What man would want her? She'd asked herself that question a thousand times over the past few years and now she'd come to the sad realization she was destined to live in this house the rest of her born days, watching the other women come and go as they found men. While she remained alone.

But maybe that was better than the

life Thanotite men offered their wife, or wives, she tried to convince herself. Maybe working like a slave to a man's will wasn't the way things were supposed to be, no matter what the Right Reverend Thatcher preached every Sunday — all day Sunday — in the church beside the cemetery filled with forgotten women. Women didn't even receive gravestones in Thanody.

You got no call thinkin' that way, she told herself. If any of the men discovered her blasphemous thoughts . . .

That was plumb foolishness. No man could hear her thoughts, not even the all-powerful Thanotite men.

But those thoughts showed in the sadness washing through her blue eyes and across her full face, didn't they? Plain as day in her reflection and she best just hide that before someone noticed.

Loneliness. Was there a sharper sword? One that could cut a soul more deeply or let you to bleed more liberally? She'd asked herself that a thousand times, too, each time she questioned — in her mind

— her leaders' admonitions and proclamations. Each time she wondered if a subservient, obedient life was preferable to a lonely one.

She still hadn't come to an answer she could bear. She supposed she might never.

But it didn't matter anyway, because men were not interested in her, except maybe some of the very old who had lost their spouses. Some of *them* weren't particular.

Maybe she should just accept one of their offers of marriage —

A noise captured her attention, pulled her from her thoughts. Some kind of disturbance, out in the street. She hadn't even noticed the three riders come in, dismount, but she noticed them now, and a gnawing fear worked through her belly. Her plump hands went to the strings of her bonnet, twisting, fingers going white. Her breath caught in her throat as one of the men slammed a fist into Traylor Prentice's jaw and sent him to the boardwalk.

Those three — *evil*, was the only word she could put to them. They looked like Mexicans, but their faces, to a man, had the cast of the Devil.

What happened next sent slivers of horror through her innards. But she couldn't take her gaze from the sight of that man hauling Prentice up and slamming him into a supporting beam. A gasp escaped her lips and her hands went to her lips. Tears welled in her eyes. Prentice was dead. She knew it, even from this distance. The way he fell, like a sack of bones . . .

She knew two of his wives.

The leader — she assumed he must be the leader, since he had killed Prentice — shouted something, and she uttered a small laugh born of nervousness, fear.

'No — no one will offer objection,' she whispered, answering the man's question, though he could not hear her, was not even aware of her presence. No one in Thanody would object. No one would lift a finger to stop these men.

Not to protect their own, nor their possessions. Not to stop what she suddenly knew was going to occur. It was scrawled across their faces. They aimed to have their way with the women in this town.

A moment later that conclusion was confirmed as one of the men, the youngest, she guessed from the looks of him, grabbed frail Martha Hanbury and dragged her toward the very home by whose window Melissa stood watching.

She backed away from the window, weakness flooding her legs and lead settling in her belly. Her gaze searched the small parlor for something to protect herself, but she knew better: no weapons were allowed in Thanody, and even had there been any she was forbidden to use one, forbidden any display of violence upon another. She doubted she could have forced herself to break that rule, even to save her own life.

The door burst open and the younger

man came in, shoving Martha before him. He slammed the door and eyed her, a peculiar look on his face. He hadn't expected her, that was plain, and didn't seem to care for the fact she was here. Martha shivered like a new-born kitten and her eyes were wide as pie plates. Tears streaked down her cheeks.

The man grabbed Martha's arm and flung her to the sofa. He stepped up next to Melissa, whipping his gun from the worn holster at his hip.

Melissa gasped, the certainty that this man was going to take her virginal gift from her rising terror in her soul.

But he didn't. He jerked up the gun, slammed her in the chin with the sidegate. Both legs went different ways and she stumbled backward. Before she could gain any control over her ragged balance she crashed to the parlor floor in front of the couch. Martha uttered a sharp cry and the man swung the gun to her.

'You go right ahead and cry and screech all you want, skinny,' he yelled, drool slithering from his mouth. 'You do that and I just might let you live, but you keep yer goddamned mouth shut when I walk out of here, you got that?'

Melissa, vision clearing, glanced at Martha, who stared at the man, uncomprehending.

'You're not — ' Melissa said, looking back to the bandit.

He uttered a strained laugh. 'I ain't, not with the likes of her, nor you. Neither of you is my type, you catch my drift . . . '

Her dazed mind couldn't rightly fathom what he meant by that, but maybe it was because she was fat and Martha was flesh hanging on bones. Whatever his rejection of them, she said a silent prayer to God above he wasn't going to soil them.

'You,' the man said, keeping the gun aimed on Martha. 'I want whatever undergarments you got on beneath that sack of a dress you're wearing. Now! And scream while you give 'em to me.'

Terror again flashed across Martha's

face and she made no move to comply.

'Goddammit, what'd I tell ya?' He pulled the trigger and thunder filled the room. Martha's frail body jumped half off the couch, then pitched forward on to the floor. She lay still. Blood pooled beneath her.

A shriek worked its way up Melissa's throat, but he swung the gun to her, chopping it short.

'Uh-uh . . . don't want to go and scream and let my kin know there's anybody else in this place, do ya? I'm givin' you the same chance I gave her. They saw me haul her skinny ass in here, so you jest get her undergarments off for me, why don't ya? 'Less you want to end up in the same condition as your friend there.'

Melissa shook her head, pure reflex. 'I don't understand . . . what you're here for.'

'I ain't got the inclination to explain it to ya, other than to say I'm a bit different than my brothers. And you're too goddamn fat and feminine to

19

interest me. Now do what I told ya, 'fore I change my mind and put a bullet in your big-assed hide.'

Melissa hesitated and he jabbed the gun forward, gritting his teeth. She crawled over to Martha, her hands shaking as she reached beneath the dead woman's skirt . . .

2

Marshal James Tredder was an old friend; that's probably the only reason Josh Dellin found himself riding into Dark Springs on a warm spring morning when he should have been sleeping off a hangover. Two days previous, he had received a telegram from his old riding partner, now lawdog in Dark Springs going on seven years. He'd not laid eyes on Tredder for all those years, and the telegram had said damn little other than 'Request Your Help'. But Josh knew it was about a job, likely one he didn't need or want at the moment; and Tredder never would have lowered himself to calling in a manhunter unless the situation was damned serious.

When they'd parted ways it was because Jim had started seeing the law different than Josh, started sticking to it like it was God-defined instead of government gospel. Before that day, they both hired out as manhunters for various cattle spreads, hell, even chased down a few errant husbands now and again. Good times that had only tallied about two years, but days Josh recollected warmly. Perhaps the only days he hadn't been truly alone since losing his family to bandits when he was a young 'un.

But Jim had started craving structure, guidelines — limitations, Josh called them — while Josh preferred the freedom and independence of the open trail. Times were, hunting down killers, he simply made his own rules and the law be damned. It had to be that way or vicious men would remain free to murder the innocent. In some cases, the law was just plain useless, to his way of thinking. The world needed men who did what needed to be done.

He shook his head, shifted in his saddle, a twinge of doubt taking him. Now that he was approaching his mid-thirties he wondered if he hadn't been the one who'd ridden the wrong trail. If maybe the lack of structure correlated with an ever-growing escape of conscience. If maybe the lines didn't get thinner, to where it became difficult to tell the difference between a vicious killer and a run-of-the-mill bank robber.

He reckoned *he* still knew the difference, but he could see where some might lose sight of that, and, beyond that, lose sight of the simple things that made life worth living.

Maybe Jim Tredder had made the smarter decision, in the end, getting out of a business where each day threatened to end your life and each night meant another in an endless string of them without stability or companionship.

Josh reckoned that was a big part of the reason for his reluctance in accepting Jim's request to come to Dark Springs. He'd been mulling over taking a break from his work, perhaps . . .

A sigh escaped his lips. Maybe that was just a foolish notion. Maybe a man couldn't escape what he was, and what was meant to be.

But was a life alone meant for a man named Josh Dellin?

Well, he had decided to come to Dark Springs, so now he was stuck with that decision — unless he turned around right quick like. But if Jim was calling on him for help that meant something went beyond the limitations of the law. And Jim Tredder wasn't a man to admit anything lay beyond the scope of the law without a hell of a reason.

Josh wagered he wasn't going to like that reason one damn bit.

He had to admit, however, it *did* rouse his manhunter's curiosity. So here he was, ass-sore from riding the roan beneath him for two days of bad trail and murderous bugs, when he could have been in some town drinking away the faces of the men he had killed in the line of duty and, worse, the faces of those who had died by their hand, the ones he hadn't been able to save.

Josh Dellin wasn't an overly large man, just a shade past five feet ten without his boots, but wiry as a mountain cat, with a hide as tough as dried leather. His face, though handsome, showed too many days under the harsh sun and the erosion of an even harsher occupation. Lines had burrowed into his forehead and about his blue eyes; he swore the dark half-circles beneath those eyes had become permanent squatters.

He let out another sigh as he entered the wide main street of Dark Springs. Just like any other little town in this part of Colorado, nestled in a backdrop of blue-painted Rockies and emerald-studded hills and forest, it was instantly forgettable.

Folks gave him passing looks as he sidled up to the boardwalk in front of a large plate glass window with the words 'Marshal's Office' arcing in gilt lettering across the glass. Those looks came friendly enough, no sense of tenseness or fear, which puzzled Josh. He'd expected some sort of obvious crisis, but outwardly Dark Springs appeared as placid as any town he'd ridden through.

He dismounted, tethered his horse to the hitch rail. Removing his battered Stetson, he swiped a forearm across his brow, mopping away sweat and trail dust that left a streak across the arm of his blue bibshirt. His back pained and he angled himself side to side as he set his hat back atop his head, working out the cricks.

'This better be worth the backache,' he murmured, stepping up on to the boardwalk.

As Josh entered the office, a man looked up from behind a large desk set to the right, near a small dust-coated window. Morning light from that window washed over the man's face and glittered from the tin star on his breast. Josh's first impression was that his former friend had aged a good twenty years, though they were roughly a year apart. Josh would have guessed that he himself would have been the haggard one, but something had taken its toll on his friend's face.

'Well, as I live and breathe!' the marshal said, lifting out of his chair like a man older than his years. 'Josh Dellin, you old scoundrel.'

Josh closed the door, doffed his hat. 'Reckon it's been a spell, hasn't it, Jim?'

The marshal came around the desk, proffering his hand. 'Reckon the hell it has, old friend.'

Tredder's grip was still iron and Josh smiled. 'Figured you'd be all tallowed and settled down by now,' Josh said.

The marshal waved Josh to a chair in front of the desk. Josh cast a glance about the room, noting the bank of three cells to the rear were empty, then lowered himself on to the hard-backed chair and tossed his hat on to the desk.

The lawdog returned to his seat behind the desk.

'Well, I'm settled, that's fact. Got me a good woman, but she can't cook worth a damn. Won't be getting tallowed that way.'

Josh smiled, but something inside envied the look of contentment that crossed his former friend's eyes when he mentioned his wife. But that look quickly passed, another replacing it: pain, perhaps mixed with defeat.

'Reckon you're the lucky one, then.' Josh's voice held no particular emotion.

'Am I?' Jim shrugged, leaned back in his chair. 'Times I find myself longing for that open trail, no restrictions on tracking down those who needed punishin'.'

Josh's brow crinkled and he studied the man, at first wondering if Jim Tredder weren't simply mocking him. Yet sincerity was scrawled across the man's face and heavy in his tone.

'Gotta tell ya, it surprises the hell out of me to hear you say that, Jim. Day you left you had your convictions set in stone.'

The marshal nodded, mood darkening. 'I did at that, didn't I?' He paused, gaze lifting to the window and a strained silence briefly pervaded the small office. 'Things change with time, don't they, Josh?'

Josh gave a casual flick of his head. 'Reckon that's a truism.'

The marshal's gaze swung back to Josh. 'That's one thing damn sure set in stone . . . or maybe in blood.'

'Only men who don't change are fools and felons, I hear tell.'

'I've changed, Josh. I've changed a lot recently.'

Josh nodded, shifted in his seat. 'I figure you must have done some soul-searchin' in order to call me in. We didn't really see eye to eye on dispensin' justice when we parted ways.'

Tredder uttered a chopped laugh. 'No, we didn't. I got my sights all focused on abiding by the law of the land and you — '

'Got my sights from Mr Colt.' Josh smiled and a bit of the tension he felt building between them released. He had half expected a lecture on holding to the law, but it was plain that wasn't going to be the case.

'You might have been the smarter of the two of us, Josh. I'm tellin' you plain.'

Josh's eyes widened a hair. 'I was just thinkin' that about you 'fore I came in here. Trail gets a mite lonesome and endless.'

'I imagine it does, but so does being shackled by rules while others break them at will.'

Josh's brow furrowed. 'Maybe it's best you tell me why you called me in, then. I got a notion it's something pretty big.'

The marshal nodded, leaned forward, then opened a drawer and pulled out a folder. He tossed it on the desk before Josh. Josh eyed the folder, then drew it towards him.

'What's this?' Josh asked, looking at the marshal, whose face was now fraught with deep lines of tension.

'You know how I felt about the law, Josh. You know for me to go lookin' to skirt it means bad business.'

Josh nodded. 'Had that figured before I walked in here.'

'I'm willin' to step outside the rules again, for the first time since the days we rode together. But I can't do it myself. I'm too set in my ways. I got a wife . . . '

'I get your meanin'. You got a job that needs doin' but the law ain't no good for it.'

'I'm willin' to surrender my notions things are set in stone and I'm willin' to look the other way . . . like we did back when we rode together.'

Josh sighed, flipped open the folder and fanned out the contents. Inside were four drawings of men, all Mexicans from the looks of them. Three younger and one an older man. He studied their features, but no recognition came from the likenesses.

'Who are they?' He looked up at the marshal.

'The Chulo brothers — Marcus, Brint and Billy — and Miguel, their father.'

31

Josh shrugged. 'Name ain't familiar. What have they done and who have they done it to?'

'More to the point, what haven't they done? The brothers go around callin' themselves the Prairie Wolves. Outwardly, they tell folks it's a family thing, that name. But a lot of folks know better.'

'They wanted?'

'Not . . . legally. That's where you come in.'

Josh shuffled the drawings back into the folder, flipped it shut. 'Maybe you best give me the details.'

The marshal leaned back, face growing tighter. 'Rape, murder. They got a thing for the ladies. After they use 'em they go around hanging their undergarments in trees, like dogs marking their territory. They, along with their pa, come out of Coyote Creek. They kill some of the women they use, depending on their mood, I reckon. Some they let live to suffer.'

Something in Josh's belly twisted.

32

'Why haven't they been brought in, if they're that out in the open?'

'Law's complicated around these parts, you know that. They've scared folks into not testifying against them, killed some who might.'

'Still don't seem like enough not to earn them a necktie party.'

'Miguel . . . he owns a hell of a lot of territory in and around Coyote Creek. Rich as all hell, mostly, I suspect, from crooked government deals and plenty of local illegal stuff that gets swept under the carpet. Has himself diplomatic immunity of some sort, from his former ambassadorship to Mexico and some friends in the governor's office, as well as a number of the town's councilmen. Marshal in Coyote Creek is likely bought and paid for, but not certain.'

'So these boys run roughshod over the town, rape and kill women there . . . '

'Mostly in the surrounding towns, way I hear tell. Miguel is careful about having too much land on his stoop. Just got a report the boys were seen around Thanody. These boys — they put the fear of death in folks, you gotta understand. They reckon they're untouchable, and until now they have been.'

Josh studied the marshal, seeing something else behind his words. 'You must have a stronger reason for compromising your principles than just that. This kind of thing goes on in towns across the west. I've seen it before.'

Jim frowned, sadness welling in his eyes. 'A personal reason. My wife's got a sister in Trallerville. I believe these boys . . . I believe they killed her, raped her first.'

Josh ran a finger over his upper lip. 'You got proof to that, witnesses?'

'No. No, I don't. I got my gut feeling and their method of operation. Her undergarments were found swinging from a tree beneath which they left her body for the buzzards.'

'Still, if we got the wrong — '

'We don't!' The marshal slammed a

fist against the desk. 'Goddammit, Josh, we never needed much more proof than that when we rode the trail. They did this thing and I swore it to my wife I'd give her sister some peace by bringing in her killers. Only I'm goddamned ashamed to admit I can't do it myself. I've gotten too comfortable, maybe. I dunno what it is. Maybe I'm just a goddamn coward.'

Josh gave him a comforting expression. 'Take it easy, Jim. I'm just askin' the questions I have to ask. Your gut feeling's good enough for me to take at least a closer look at them.'

'I don't want a goddamn closer look, Josh. I want them dead. They killed my sister-in-law. They violated her. That don't mean a hell of lot to some of the menfolk out here, but it does to me.'

Josh nodded. 'Does to me too, I reckon. And I understand damn well that if you didn't believe this with everything in your soul you wouldn't have called in someone like me, you wouldn't have bent your principles. But

I gotta wonder what I can do against men protected by a town. I can't just walk in and put bullets in them. And if I bring them in — '

'They just walk out again, grinning like the Devil was on their side. Then they take some other poor woman and do to her what they did to my wife's sister. Maybe someday their luck will run out, but it won't be today or tomorrow or maybe even ten years from now unless something gets done.'

Josh sighed, then stood. He grabbed his hat from the desk and set it atop his head. The marshal eyed him with a pleading look, one laced with deep sadness, sadness for a wife's sister tragically murdered and sadness for convictions he'd once held as silver that had now tarnished.

'I'll ride out to Thanody, take a look-see. Then maybe head on up to Coyote Creek. I can't promise . . . '

'Please, Josh. Only man in this goddamned world a promise means anything from is you, I figure.' The marshal stood, leaned heavily against his desk.

Josh frowned. 'This Thanody, know anything about it?'

The marshal's voice trembled. 'Sect of religious types runs it. Hear tell they're non-violent to the extreme, marry multiple wives.'

'Like one ain't enough.' Josh grinned, hoping to lighten his friend's mood.

'Please, Josh. These men . . . they're monsters.'

Josh went to the door, gripped the door handle, squeezed it until his knuckles bleached. Christ, he should have just stayed drunk, but what it must have taken for the man behind that desk to come to him — maybe he owed it to a friendship that had been or maybe he was just plain loco but he said: 'All right, Jim. I'll give you my word. If these men are guilty they will pay for what they did.'

'They're guilty. And they'll keep on being guilty till they're in the ground.'

Josh nodded, opened the door,

looked back to the marshal. 'We had some good times, didn't we? Back in those days?'

A hint of a smile crossed the marshal's lips. 'We sure as hell did, old friend.'

Josh stepped out on to the boardwalk, pulling the door closed behind him. He'd agreed to do a job for an old friend but deep inside he mourned for something that was lost between them, something that would never live again. They were different people, now, and he was hard-pressed to say which of them life had battered the most. For the first time in a long time, he suspected it wasn't him.

3

Two hours later Josh Dellin was on the trail again, riding towards Thanody. He'd spent a couple of hours cleaning up with a shave and a birdbath, working the kinks out his legs and back, then devoured a quick breakfast of bacon, eggs and fried potatoes before heading out of Dark Springs.

Each time he began to have second thoughts about the case — it wasn't a simple matter of chasing down a man or men who had Wanted dodgers and rewards tacked to their hides — the memory of Jim Tredder's face haunted his mind. The man back in that office, that wasn't the Tredder he had known years ago. This Tredder was a man defeated by life, one who'd come to the realization everything he'd held as gospel had deserted him.

In a way, Josh felt his friend's pain,

because fact was, he'd wrestled with those very same feelings for a spell now. How many nights had he wondered while he lay alone, staring up at the ceiling in some dingy hotel room in some town that was just like every other town, if the convictions he'd clung to so passionately were the right ones? If he'd made the correct choice when he and Tredder parted ways, and, if he had made the right one, whether what he did wasn't somehow as bad as the deeds of the men he tracked down?

The man he used to be had been so goddamned certain he knew everything. No one could have told him he was wrong; he knew his decision was right and just — and, most of all, *necessary*. But as he'd grown older . . . well, maybe everything was no longer so black and white. Maybe the world — the West — had turned to gray. Maybe Jim Tredder had come to see that as well, but with a notion that it made years of his life a lie.

For Josh perhaps it didn't mean his

life had been a lie; perhaps it just meant it was something whose time had passed, or, more accurately, something that needed amending.

You really want to quit doing this? he asked himself, the thought giving his belly a twist, though it wasn't the first time he'd entertained such a notion. Did he really want to let men the law couldn't touch keep on doin' what they were doin'? Murdering. Raping. Taking what wasn't theirs. Like these Prairie Wolves Tredder had told him about?

It wasn't that easy to let go of everything he had been. It wasn't a simple matter of just stopping. And when it came down to it what real reason did he have to give it up? Where would he go, what would he do? *Maybe a small ranch somewhere . . .*

He almost laughed but the roan hit a bump on the forest-flanked trail and snapped his teeth together.

The thought of settling down . . . it was a right fine dream, wasn't it? But just as lonely as the life he now led without someone with whom to share it.

He'd had women. Plenty of 'em, truth to tell. Some of them bought and paid for with earnings from his manhunting cases, and others eager to bed a man with a reputation for stopping the guilty with the Peacemaker holstered at his hip in some peculiar type of hero worship he didn't rightly understand. But he envied Tredder in a way, because Tredder had a woman whose love obviously mattered so much to him he'd abandoned his convictions to give her a measure of peace by bringing her sister's killers to justice — in any way necessary.

Josh had never known that kind of love, and reckoned he never would. Maybe such a thing wasn't possible for men such as he, men who lived by the gun, rode by the bullet and confined themselves to a solitary and dangerous life by necessity and choice.

Hell, it didn't matter at the moment, did it? He'd given Tredder his word and maybe he'd be lucky enough to get himself killed this time and save his troubled mind the duty of a decision.

This time he did utter a small chuckle, but the expression held no humor, only irony.

The trail widened and a few hundred yards on he spotted the town, Thanody. A half-circular affair of simple buildings awash in late-morning sunlight, it appeared peaceful from the distance.

Yet still a shiver trickled through him. Something unseen, dark, that manhunter's sixth sense, told him something was wrong.

His hands tightened on the reins, knuckles going white. *You got no reason for such a feeling*, he told himself, and tried to shake off the sensation, but could not. He'd come to trust that manhunter's sixth sense over the years; those feelings were seldom wrong.

'Something's happened,' he whispered.

As he reached the entrance to the

town, he spotted few folks moving about the boardwalk, those doing so seemingly as if in some sort of a trance. They sauntered towards their destinations, as if programmed to do so by years of practice, repetition, but not motivation. The men all wore the same heavy trousers and white shirts, and most of them sported beards and wore flat hats. The women all wore heavy woolen skirts and low-pulled, over-large bonnets.

The day had heated up, a premonition of the coming summer. Sweat had soaked both his underarms and dripped from his brow to run down his face. Such heavy clothing from the town's dwellers told him they wore it more as a uniform than for comfort or function.

Tugging the reins, he slowed his horse to a walk, noticing the few townsfolk who glanced his way did so with fear shimmering in their eyes and muscles tightening on their faces. That solidified the dark feeling crawling through his innards.

Something had indeed happened, and it wasn't something good.

Women, stopping and turning to gaze his way, their heads held low, suddenly whirled and vanished into buildings.

'Dammit,' he muttered under his breath, gut sinking as a notion flickered through his mind. 'I'm too goddamn late . . . '

An instant later his notion that the men he sought, the Chulo brothers, had visited Thanody was confirmed as his gaze rose to a tree in the center of town. From that tree hung numerous women's undergarments. They swayed in the warm breeze, like perverse white flags that silently spoke of forced surrender.

A heavy footfall came from the boardwalk to the left and Josh's attention shifted from the tree to a man who had stopped on the boardwalk. Josh reined up, peered at the fellow, whose bearded face showed signs of fear. A nervous tick stuttered at his left eye and balls of muscle quivered to either side of his jaw.

'What do you want here?' the man asked, his voice carrying a slight tremble but also bitterness. Others on the boardwalk stopped, looked Josh's way.

'Who are you?' Josh asked, not particularly taken with the man's tone.

'I am one of the church leaders in this town, Josiah Herridge. Who are you, sir?'

Josh glanced at the other men, noting none of them carried guns or the looks of fellows intending to make a hostile move. They simply looked more scared than anything else.

Before he answered, his gaze swept from the men to the rooftops, to corners of clapboard and brick buildings, to doorways, searching for a glint of sunlight on metal, or furtive motion, anything that might indicate any of the Chulo brothers were still in town. Although these men weren't heeled, others might have remained behind who might be armed, and he made a fine target, sitting in the middle of the street atop his horse.

He spotted nothing, but remained alert as he looked back to the man.

'Name's Josh Dellin. Passin' through here on my way to Coyote Creek. Lookin' for some men. Perhaps you mighta seen them.'

The man shook his head too quickly. 'Those men are not here, so please be on your way.'

Josh's brow furrowed. 'Somethin' tells me you know exactly which men I mean.'

The man's face tightened, and anger flashed in his eyes. 'It does not matter. Those men are not here. It would please us if you were not as well.'

'Right neighborly of you.' Josh's gaze shifted back to the tree and under-garments, then went again to Herridge. 'But I reckon you got a damned good reason for not being hospitable, don't you?'

'As I told you, it does not matter. They are not here.'

'But they were here, weren't they?'

Josh's eyes locked with Herridge's.

The man shifted feet, discomfort in his stance. 'They are not here.'

Josh nodded, frustration crawling through his nerves. 'Established that. But 'less you're decorating your tree with undergarments for an early Christmas, it's obvious they paid you a call. Not a goddamn social call, either.'

The man's head lowered and his gaze went to the boardwalk, then, moments later, came back up. 'They were here. They are no longer. It does not matter.'

'You keep sayin' that, but reckon it matters to me. Reckon it matters to a woman whose sister they killed in Dark Springs and reckon it might matter to some of the women in this here town, too.'

The man's carriage stiffened. 'What's done is done.'

'Maybe so, but I aim to see to it what's done is paid for.'

'We are a non-violent town, Mr Dellin.'

Josh's gaze drilled the man. 'That

what you told the Chulos?'

The man's eyes narrowed. 'They were told. They murdered one of our leaders.'

'And your women?'

Herridge shifted feet and swallowed hard. 'Some of them were — '

John nodded. 'Any killed?'

'Two. Another taken.'

'Taken?'

'Tilly Mathews. They took her with them.'

With a sigh, Josh's gaze swept back to the tree then towards the opposite end of town. 'Any of you go after her?'

'They would have killed us.' Herridge's voice came weak, not quite ashamed, but more worried about judgment by someone not of their group.

Josh's gaze swung back to the bearded man. 'So you just let them ride off with one of your own?'

'The Lord will decide her fate, Mr Dellin. It is not for us to raise weapons or fists against other men.'

Something in the way Herridge said

'men' made Josh's belly knot and he wasn't entirely certain what it was. 'Wish to hell I understood that, Mr Herridge, I truly do. But right now I'm having a hard time thinkin' about some poor girl in the hands of men like these.'

'Women are made for a man's need, for procreation. They are lower creatures, much like the animals in the field. It is no different than if those men had taken one of our horses or cattle. We can replace them.'

Josh tensed, a surge of fury washing through him as he suddenly understood what the man's inflection had meant a moment before. Josh might have begrudgingly respected the man's conviction for non-violence against others, but others did not include women, and any scrap of respect he might have had for him perished.

'Much as that disgusts me, Mr Herridge, I reckon it ain't my place to make judgments on whatever it is you got here in this town. But it is my place to find those men and you got any information that helps me do that faster you best be out with it. While I do consider myself a tolerant man that don't mean I'm a particularly patient one.'

A certain hardness came into Herridge's eyes. 'I can tell you nothing other than they came in and did what they did, then rode out again.'

'With one of your women.'

'We have others . . . '

Josh had developed a deep dislike for Herridge and every word the man uttered put another nail in that coffin. He had half an urge to show the man a little violence in the form of throttling him but refrained. It would do no good and he had encountered the man's type before. So rigid in their beliefs and absolute in their viewpoint they could see things no other way.

Christ, maybe you're a bit like that yourself, Dellin . . .

Maybe, but one thing he did not do was view another person as a possession.

'Why is that underwear still in the tree?' Josh asked, suppressing his anger for the moment. 'Why the hell haven't you removed it?'

'They told us not to.' Simple and absolute. Like a child who'd been told to stay in his room or face a switch.

Josh scoffed. 'They told you not to? And you do everything everybody tells ya, I take it?'

Crimson flooded the man's cheeks. He may have practiced non-violence but anger was still an option. 'They threatened to come back if we removed it.'

'Got news for you, Herridge. Those men are coming back anyway 'cause you made it so goddamn easy for them. That underwear is just marking their territory like randy coyotes. You got any notions they'll stay clear you best revise them.'

Fear wiped the anger from the man's features. He clearly knew what Josh had told him was the truth. 'Please, sir, ride out and leave us be.'

Josh sighed. 'I aim to do just that, Mr Herridge. If you see me again I hope it's 'cause I'm bringing your kidnapped girl back alive . . . but I got my doubts. Maybe you can think about that a spell and see her face 'fore you fall asleep at night.'

'She was just a woman . . . ' The man shrugged and the expression sent fury through Josh's veins, but he reckoned it was a lost cause.

His gaze swept to some of the other men, seeing their expressions hadn't changed. All held fear, and the hope that he would simply ride out and leave them to their lives as they wished them to be was mirrored on their faces.

'How 'bout the rest of you?' Josh said, lifting his voice. 'Any of you got a mind to ride with me after your girl?'

None made a move to speak, and he nodded.

'That's about what I figured,' Josh said, voice lowering. He looked back to Herridge. 'There's a fine line between conviction and cowardice, Mr Herridge.

I reckon you know in your heart you crossed it.'

'You do not understand our ways, Mr Dellin. What our people have gone through. We know what is right.'

A pang of memory stabbed Josh's mind. He recollected a conversation not so different many years ago when he and Tredder rode their separate ways.

'You're right, I don't understand them. Reckon I never will and don't care to. Reckon you might take it from someone who knows, though, black ain't always black and white ain't always white . . . '

'I'll go with you — ' A voice came from his left and he twisted in the saddle to see a heavyset woman coming from the opposite boardwalk into the street. She'd come from a small house whose door now lay open.

'Melissa!' Herridge said, fire in his tone. 'Go back to your home. You have not been given permission to speak here.'

Josh flashed Herridge a corrosive look. 'Reckon she don't need your permission.' He looked back to the girl. 'You see the men who did this?'

The young woman glanced at Herridge, fear rampant in her eyes. For a moment Josh thought she might turn and run back into the house. Whatever hold these men had over their women it was a right powerful one and likely came with a wagonload of hell and damnation.

'I-I saw them,' she said at last, her voice unsteady, eyelids fluttering. 'I watched one of them kill Martha. He made me take off her . . . her undergarments and give them to him.'

Josh glanced back at Herridge, whose face appeared almost purple. 'You got a place that rents horses?'

Herridge didn't answer. His gaze traveled back to the young woman, and she backed up a step. 'You'll be punished for this, Melissa. Go back to your home. Now.'

Josh uttered a low laugh. 'Gotta wonder how such a non-violent man punishes folks for disobedience, Mr Herridge.'

'We have our methods. Melissa knows them well.'

'Don't figure I care much for the sound of that, Herridge. She's coming with me . . . if she wants to.'

'I forbid you to take her!' Herridge said.

'Now that's right funny, because I don't see how a non-violent man such as yourself might stop me. 'Less you got some balls in those britches some-where . . .'

Veins pulsated at Herridge's temples but he didn't say anything further.

Josh turned his attention back to the young woman. 'I'll ask you, then . . . there a place to rent a horse in this town?'

Her gaze shifted to Herridge and her entire frame shuddered visibly. Josh could tell she was one step away from changing her mind and running back to her house.

'I — maybe I shouldn't,' she said, face reddening.

Josh nodded. 'Unlike your leader

here, I'm offerin' you that choice. You can come or stay, but I got a feeling you couldn't live with yourself if you let those men kill that poor girl way they killed your friend.'

She looked at the ground for long moments. When she looked up her cheeks were flushed with scarlet and tears shimmered in her eyes. 'I'll go. That girl they took . . . she lived with me and Martha. She was so young . . . '

Josh nodded. He fished in a pocket, pulled out a wad of greenbacks and tossed them to the young woman. 'Fetch a horse — I assume you can ride?'

'I can ride.'

'Melissa!' Herridge snapped. 'It is forbidden for women to ride the animals. It is unclean. You know this!'

The young woman shivered under the man's tone, but turned and started towards a livery halfway down the street. Josh had a notion he'd have to insist whoever ran the livery rent a horse to her, but he gave Herridge a final look.

'You got a goddamned funny notion of what's unclean, Herridge. Especially with the blood on your hands if that girl is dead.'

'I had nothing to do with those men taking her.' An indignant edge seeped into the man's voice. Spittle had gathered at the corners of his mouth. He was someone used to total control and right now with what had happened in this town and with the young woman's defiance, that was all coming apart for him. In that instant Josh saw not a man of conviction and faith, but one craving of power and obedience because of some insecurity lurking within himself.

'Maybe you didn't give them the key but you showed them the door, Mr Herridge.'

Josh swung around and heeled his horse into a trot after the young woman, who'd already reached the livery.

'You are in defiance of the laws of God, Mr Dellin!' Herridge yelled behind him. 'Sinner! Blasphemer! You will both burn in Hell for such insolence and disobedience! Mark my word, sir! Mark my word!'

Josh glanced back at him, wondering if the man would have felt so brave yelling that at a Chulo brother. A weary expression pulled at his lips. 'As the saying goes, Mr Herridge, I'll have myself a passelful of company . . . '

4

Josh Dellin had argued with the livery owner for nearly an hour before the man agreed to rent a horse to Melissa, whose last name he'd discovered in the course of the exchange was Gatner. For while the fine folks of Thanody weren't inclined toward violence, endless arguing didn't rank on their lists of sins.

The argument ended only after Josh agreed to purchase the animal, a whey-bellied bay, for five dollars more than it was worth.

He'd begun to debate the wisdom of the expense and bringing the girl along at all, because it would make her a target and that might outweigh the fact she was the only witness he might get to testify to the heinous acts committed by the Chulo brothers. But what was done was done, and it was now his responsibility to protect the young woman riding beside him.

They rode the tree-lined trail towards Coyote Creek, which was roughly a few hours' ride distant at their present pace, the young woman silent beside him. Her horse, being what it was, necessitated slower travel than he cared for, but just the fact someone was riding beside him for the first time since Tredder and he had gone their separate ways gave him a peculiar feeling in the pit of his belly. The fact she was a woman wasn't lost on him, either.

'You know going back to Thanody after defying Herridge might be a problem,' he said, at a loss for casual conversation.

The girl kept staring straight ahead, but nodded. 'I cannot go back without accepting punishment.'

Her voice was sweet, light, like church bells. He noted with a certain amount of interest that he'd never taken in the sound of a woman's tone before. Normally the women he bedded weren't a wellspring of conversation and a half-drunk randy fella didn't pay much attention to anything but whispered vulgarities and saucy promises. The thought of it filled him with an awkward sensation and he shifted in the saddle, licked his lips.

'I don't figure that,' he said. 'You're doin' what's right. Your town leaders trying to stop that, well, that's just plain wrong, way I see it.'

'The town leaders are only looking out for the betterment of all, Mr Dellin. I'm sure they have their reasons.' He heard far less conviction in her voice than he had in Herridge's proclamations. She was defending them out of pure reflex, not staunch belief.

He glanced at her. 'Why do I get the notion you ain't entirely convinced of that.'

Her expression didn't change. 'I . . . used to be. Sometimes . . . sometimes now I wonder.'

It was hard for her to admit, he could tell. She wasn't used to expressing her notions to anyone, other than herself, perhaps.

'Life comes with questions, Miss Gatner. Those who don't question are fools or plumb loco.'

Weren't you that way not so long ago, Dellin? Did you ever question your duty, your mission? That make you the fool or just crazy?

'I have a notion you're mocking our beliefs, Mr Dellin.' No anger or accusation came with her tone. She just seemed . . . lifeless, maybe. He wondered if she weren't suffering some sort of shock caused by seeing her friend murdered.

'No, ma'am, I'm not mocking them. I'm for anything that leads to the betterment of everyone, but the men in your town' — he paused, gaze shifting to her, then back to the trail ahead — 'seems to me they're only interested in the betterment of themselves. Reckon to the detriment of you womenfolk.'

She glanced at him for the first time, something in her eyes saying she had questioned that very thing. 'Is there a different way, Mr Dellin? All I see is violence everywhere, killing. Blood runs freely but ideas do not. All I see are men like those outlaws who came to Thanody.'

He had a desire to tell her he didn't see ideas flowing freely in Thanody, either, but refrained. 'Those men came into Thanody regardless of your beliefs, maybe even because those beliefs made your town an easy target. Which ain't makin' a judgment on those beliefs being right or wrong, just statin' a fact. There'll always be men like the Chulos, animals who think they can just take whatever they want at the expense of others' lives and liberty. No belief will stop that.'

'But we can stop ourselves from hurting others, can we not?' Her gaze remained fixed on the trail.

'Reckon you can stop hurting others with your fists. But can you stop doing it with your words? Sometimes words carry more violence than a blow, ma'am. Can you tell me what your leaders are doing to their womenfolk isn't hurting them worse than striking them physically?'

He glanced at her, saw her body stiffen. She'd asked herself the question, perhaps many times; he didn't have to be a crystal gazer to be certain of it.

'Things are the way they are, Mr Dellin.'

'Call me Josh, ma'am.'

'If you'll call me Melissa. I may be unwed but I'm not a ma'am.'

He nodded, hearing pain bleed into her tone. 'Reckon if things were set in stone you wouldn't be riding with me.'

'Perhaps you're right, Mr — Josh. Maybe I just haven't listened to God in too long.'

He uttered a small laugh. 'Or maybe you just started.'

She flashed him a look that carried no anger, only a wonder whether he might be right.

They rode for another half hour in silence, Josh debating how much to question her about what had occurred in Thanody, if she were ready to relive it. The thoughts came with a bit of frustration because he found he was a damn poor judge of female character. All the women he'd known were of the type that came and went; times were many he was damn lucky even to learn their names.

The day had grown even warmer, the sun arcing high overhead in a sapphire sky, beating on the leather of his saddle. Sweat trickled from beneath his arms and made his hair sticky beneath his Stetson. The scents of pine, late spring flowers and dust filled his nostrils. The breeze had grown nearly stagnant. Somewhere in the woodland birds chirped and cawed and perhaps under other circumstances he might have found it calming. But at the moment it only rode his nerves, because it felt mocking. Like the silence of death.

A young woman was out there, in the hands of men — *monsters*, he amended — and if he didn't find her soon, he reckoned he'd be lucky to bring back even a body.

'Ain't you hot in those heavy clothes?' he asked after another few minutes, trying to get his mind off the dark feeling roiling in his belly.

'It is what we are required to wear,' she said matter-of-factly.

''Fraid I need to ask you some questions that may not be the easiest to hear.'

'I've been expecting you would.'

'Those men who came in, you'll recognize them all when we come across them? Or just the one?'

'I'll recognize all of them. I saw them in the street, and the young one up close.'

'You willin' to swear to it in a court of law if I can bring them in?'

She glanced at him. 'If?'

He swallowed, knowing his line of work wasn't going to play well against her vow of non-violence. 'Sometimes I kill the men I go after, Melissa. Sometimes I ain't got a choice. These men are vicious killers. Reckon I don't have to tell you that. They might not be inclined to come peaceably.'

She tensed and he could tell she was thinking it over. 'There's more to it than that, isn't there? Something about these men.'

A sudden admiration for the young woman took hold of him. She could read a man far better than he could read a woman.

'They're protected in Coyote Creek, by their father. He owns half the town and has a lot of influence in high places. And a measure of immunity granted by a position he once held.'

'So you're telling me that even if we find these men and bring them to justice, even if I testify against them, they might still go free?'

He sighed, nodded. 'Yes, I reckon that's a strong possibility. I'm saying it's a damn difficult trail and you have to be prepared to ride it.'

'And if they walk free . . . they'll come after me, won't they?' Fear trickled into her voice, but she appeared steeled for his answer.

'Won't lie to you. They will most likely. But it won't come to that.'

She peered at him, questioning with her eyes, then figuring it out. 'You'll kill them . . . '

'I'll invite them to choose confession,' he said, knowing it amounted to the same but something about the way she said it made him want to soften his words.

'Reckon a few days ago I wouldn't have understood how a man could take the life of another . . . but after seeing what that man did to Martha . . . maybe things aren't so black and white . . . '

His belly clutched at hearing his own thoughts spoken back to him by another.

'Did that man — ?' He struggled for a way to phrase it, coming up empty. He saw no way other than asking her directly, but she saved him the trouble.

'No, he did not soil me.'

He couldn't suppress the relief that washed through him. 'You got a notion why he didn't?'

'First I thought it was because I'm fat.' Her tone came with pain, otherwise he might have let out an inappropriate chuckle.

'You ain't fat,' he said before he could stop himself.

She uttered a resigned laugh. 'The men in Thanody like their women sturdy and sleek, like a fine horse. I'm unmarried because I don't meet their standards and I'm likely to stay as such, unless I decide to accept an offer from one of the older widowers. I'm not attractive to anyone else.'

Christ, she was serious; he heard it in her tone. And he couldn't figure it. Truth to tell, the soft sweet lines of her face, the crystal blue of her eyes and wisps of strawberry-blonde hair trickling from beneath her bonnet made him uncomfortable as hell. He couldn't recollect ever seeing a lovelier woman.

'You're plump in the right places, way I see it.' It came out before he could think about it and he felt an immediate urge to shrink in his saddle.

What a goddamned foolish thing to say! he scolded himself.

She gave him an easy laugh, maybe the most honest and unbidden emotion she'd shown since they'd ridden out of Thanody.

'Reckon I'll take that as a compliment.' Her tone carried a lilt that sent a shiver through his innards.

'Meant it as such. I'm not the most eloquent of men to come down the trail, I reckon. But the men in Thanody got a lot of foolish notions to my way of thinkin' and if they can't see the beauty in a woman like you that's just one more to add to the book.'

There he went again, saying something like an idiotic, infatuated child and he couldn't figure what possessed him. He'd never been inclined to talk to women that way.

A thin smile pulled at Melissa's full lips. 'Perhaps you have some eloquence after all.'

He shifted in the saddle, struggled to get the subject back on the trail.

'Reckon we established he didn't leave you alone 'cause you're . . . uh . . . '

'Fat,' she said. 'That's what I thought at first. I always think that, I reckon. Been told it for so long . . . but I think there was another reason.'

'That reason being?'

'I don't think he likes women at all. He killed Martha but he wasn't going to use her, either. And he didn't seem to want the other men to know about it.'

Josh nodded. 'I've seen it before. Maybe in this case we can be thankful for it. This girl they took, you got a notion why, other than the obvious?'

Her lips drew into a hard line. 'Heard them say she was their insurance no one would testify against them.'

'Don't see how that would work in your town's case, way the men think about women.'

'Those men could have saved themselves the trouble,' she said, nodding. 'No one would testify. She's just a woman and the menfolk won't risk themselves for her.'

The woodland to either side of the trail began to thin after another fifteen minutes of riding, stands of trees growing farther apart, brush and boulders studding the hillsides. The trail grew more rutted, gouged by wagon wheels and the countless hoofs that had traversed it.

Melissa suddenly gasped and he didn't have to ask the reason. He had spotted the same thing she had, at the exact same instant.

Nausea surged through his belly and he had all he could do to hold it down. He had seen some terrible things in his years chasing down owlhoots, atrocious deeds, soulless men, but this . . . this was like nothing even remotely human.

Tears streaked down Melissa's face and a sob shuddered her body. A shiver swept down his spine, despite the heat, and he fought to keep himself together as they approached a stand of cotton-woods to the right of the trail.

A body hung in one of the trees,

nude, impaled on a jagged shard of branch about five feet off the ground.

A young woman's body.

He drew up, legs shaky as he climbed from his horse. He was conscious of Melissa doing the same, though she clung to the saddle when she reached the ground to keep from collapsing.

He went to the dead woman, gently grasping her, and despite the revulsion surging in his being, pulled her from the shard, then lowered her gently to the ground. Behind him he could hear Melissa retching, vomiting, and could barely stop himself from doing the same.

'Oh, Christ!' he whispered.

After staggering back to his horse, he pulled loose a blanket, then went back to the corpse and covered it. He noted the young woman's face had frozen in utter terror, her eyes wide open, her mouth frozen in a silent scream. Buzzards and insects had already begun to work on the corpse, attracted by the blood from the branch wound and from

74

a higher gunshot hole just above her left breast. His fingertips drifted over her eyes, closing the lids, but he could not force the sight of the terror-filled stare from his mind.

A scuffing sound from beside him told him Melissa had come up and he glanced up at her. She stared down at the girl's face, tears streaming from her own eyes and her entire body quaking.

'How could they — ' she said, her words trembling with horror, with utter sadness.

'Monsters. Not men.' He shook his head, then pulled the blanket over the girl's face. 'They shot her first, though that ain't a hell of a lot of consolation.'

He came to his feet, having all he could do to keep from collapsing. Maybe the Chulos had just made his world black and white again.

'Why would they do this?' Melissa asked, wrapping her arms about herself and shuddering. 'She was only seventeen.'

'Men like these, they use fear to keep

folks from lifting a finger against them. They left her as a warning in case anyone followed from Thanody, unlikely as that would be.'

Time dragged, and though he reckoned only a few minutes passed it felt like an eternity. He doubted he'd ever get the sight of the murdered girl out of his nightmares. Any qualms he might have had about going on this mission, for promising Tredder he'd bring these men down, had vanished.

'We can bring her back to Thanody,' he said after a few minutes.

'They would put her in an unmarked grave, way they do all the women.'

He nodded, the sick feeling in his belly worsening. 'We'll bring her to Coyote Creek, then. I'll see she's buried proper and maybe if the lawdog there gets a look at her he might be inclined to be more helpful against these boys, though I ain't got high hopes.'

She nodded, tears running through her fingers, which were now pressed hard against her lips.

He rolled the young woman in the blanket, then carried her to Melissa's bay and draped her corpse over the saddle. Coyote Creek, he estimated, was another few miles, so they would have to ride double on his horse.

Ten minutes saw them underway and if there was any slight comfort in the events that had turned such a devilish way, it was the feeling of Melissa pressed against his back, her arms about his waist. Some tragedies in life could only be soothed by the closeness of another human being and senseless death was one of them.

5

The letters in gilt arcing across the window said: JEBEDIAH THATCH, CABINETS AND COFFINS, and two hours later found Josh Dellin and Melissa Gatner leaving the small shop. Josh had arranged for the murdered girl's burial and paid all costs, but he reckoned that would do little to give her memory peace as long as the men who had committed such a horrible act remained free.

Nausea still twisted in his belly and he had a difficult time getting the sight of that girl's body hanging from the tree out of his mind. Tracks of tears stained Melissa's cheeks and she remained silent as she walked along the board-walk beside him.

'We'll go to the marshal,' Josh said, 'though I got a notion it won't do us much good. I aim to bring those boys in, now that I got a witness, but I'm bettin' he won't hold 'em.'

Melissa nodded, face grim, pale. 'They aren't likely just to come along peaceably.'

'No, they ain't. And once they see you — I won't sugarcoat it — your life will be in danger.'

'I accept that, but I aim to do what's right.' Her carriage stiffened with conviction and when he glanced at her, the determination showed in her eyes. The young woman's corpse had solidified her resolve.

Coyote Creek was a large town, nestled between a panorama of distant mountains, lush forest and brush-studded hillsides. A lattice-work of streets with plentiful law and business offices, saloons and shops, the town boasted its influx of men of means brought by the laying of railtrack along its southern boundary. Men like Miguel Chulo, men who had garnered prosperity by means questionable as well as legal, thrived in such places. Josh had seen it numerous times in his career, mostly from cattle barons and gold and silver magnates. Chulo had likely set himself up a nice little kingdom and considered himself untouchable. Josh hoped to change that point of view. At least where Chulo's sons were concerned.

But he didn't relish the task. Chulo would have the best lawyers in his silk pockets, and perhaps even hired guns. The moment Josh tried to toss one of his sons in a cell, the gauntlet would be thrown down and Josh and Melissa would be two against an entrenched political machine.

But just getting any of the Chulo brothers into a cell was problematic, since the local law likely rode shotgun to the senior Chulo's whims.

Folks roamed the boardwalks, women in fancy dresses and men in frock coats or ranch clothing. Yet, despite the outward appearance of serenity and prosperity, Josh noticed a dark undercurrent running through the town. Many faces held a certain tenseness, one that came from fear, or perhaps domination.

That would make his job even harder, he reckoned. Folks who lived in fear or under control reacted in peculiar ways sometimes, ways opposing their plight. They cowered, accepted things — sometimes even atrocities — free men did not.

The more he studied their faces, the more he concluded bringing the Chulo brothers in was an unlikely scenario. They would not submit to arrest, even if the marshal for some reason wasn't bought and paid for, and it was damned unlikely any support would come from the townsfolk.

'Way I see it I'm caught between a rock and hard place,' he said, voice low as they stepped off the boardwalk to cross in front of an alley.

Melissa nodded, as if knowing exactly what he was thinking. 'These people . . . I've seen the same looks on their faces as on some of the women in Thanody.'

'Reckon that might tell you some-thing . . . '

'Tells me the more I see the less I know,' she whispered. 'Less I know the more I want to run from who I've been.'

'Reckon I feel the same way most days as of late — '

The words ended with a sharp crack as something crashed into his jaw. His attention focused on Melissa and his worries over the Chulos, he hadn't been paying attention to the alley they were passing before. He'd let his guard down, something that often proved fatal for manhunters on the chase.

His legs buckled as he stumbled sideways, then down. He hit the ground hard on his side, the street spinning before his blurred vision. His hat flew into the dirt. Dazed, he didn't know what had hit him, but it was solid, metal most like, and his first suspicion was that it was a gun butt.

Melissa's small bleat of terror pene-trated the ringing in his ears, then came a man's voice:

'Well, lookee here, Brint, one of them fine ladies of Thanody has come to pay us a visit. Mighty friendly of her, wouldn't ya say?'

A second voice replied, 'Reckon you're goddamn right, Billy boy. She must've missed our special brand of lovin' and come a'lookin' for some more.'

Brint . . . Billy . . . Chulo. The truth cleared some of the cobwebs from Josh's mind and his vision struggled to focus on the two men standing over him. Melissa stood just off to the side, looking paralyzed, her eyes wide as she stared at the two brothers.

The gunmetal taste of blood soured his mouth and he spat into the dust. Pain rang through his entire jaw and his teeth throbbed. He'd be lucky if his jaw wasn't broken.

He propped himself up on to an elbow, jammed a palm against the dirt and tried to push himself to hands and knees. Sharp pain slammed into his ribs as the one called Brint buried his boot-heel in Josh's side. Josh tumbled over on to his back, gasping for the breath that had been kicked out of him. Brint reached down, snatched the Peacemaker from Josh's holster, then jammed it into his own belt.

'Reckon that's a downright nice piece you got there. Think I'll keep it.'

Billy uttered a harsh laugh and started for Melissa, who was still riveted where she stood. He grabbed her, but didn't make a move to do anything any further.

Anger sending adrenaline surging through his veins, Josh summoned whatever strength he had left and rolled over, shoving against the ground. Agony radiated through every fiber of his body as he came to his feet, unsteady, blood dribbling from his lips.

'What the hell you waitin' on, Billy?' Brint asked, tone taunting. 'I'm beginnin' to think Marcus might be right about you!'

Billy let out a curse. 'I ain't partial to fat gals, Brint, that's all! You know I like my gals skinny.'

'I ain't even goddamn sure you like your gals, Billy boy. But, hell, any port in a storm for me. Lemme at her.'

Josh lounged at Brint as he stepped toward Melissa. Off-balance, stumbling, he hit the Chulo brother, but without much power. Brint side-stepped, obviously keeping watch from the corner of his eye and expecting the move. He buried a fist in Josh's abdomen.

Josh doubled, nausea surging into his throat. Brint followed up with a blow to the side of Josh's head that sent him reeling sideways. He hit something and his legs went out from under him. He came down with a splash of dust-and-fly-dirtied water, knew he'd landed in a trough.

Billy's laugh resounded through the street and Brint turned his attention back toward Melissa, grabbing her from Billy and whirling her around.

'Now let's see if all that extra cushion's worth the pushin,' he said. 'Then maybe we'll give you what we gave that other gal we took with us. Told you folks not to come lookin' for us.'

'That'll be enough, Brint,' a voice came from the boardwalk.

Josh struggled to hoist himself out of the trough, his arms and legs refusing to work quite right. He hung over the side, panting, pain immobilizing him for the moment.

A marshal stood on the boardwalk, dull green eyes locked on Brint Chulo. Josh's vision cleared, focused on the lawdog. He was middle-aged, with a chimney sweep mustache. His frame carried too much weight in the belly and he had the look of a worn man.

'Hell, Barsten, we was just havin' ourselves a little fun!' Billy said.

Barsten's gaze shifted to the younger Chulo, then went back to Brint. 'Let her go, Brint. You know your pa wouldn't appreciate your kind of fun on his doorstep.'

Brint glared, but released Melissa, who staggered back a couple of steps.

She appeared on the verge of fainting, but somehow held her feet.

Brint stepped on to the boardwalk, not taking his gaze off the lawdog. 'You don't forget who owns this town, Barsten.'

The marshal frowned. 'I ain't forgettin'. That's why I'm stopping this. You boys might have your way more often than I got a stomach for but your pa made it plain he didn't want any' — the marshal glanced at Melissa — '*incidents* in plain sight of Coyote Creek's folks. They might look the other way when things happen in other towns, but you never know how a fella's going to react when it threatens his own.'

Brint laughed, a dark tone. 'Out of sight out of mind, that the way, Marshal?'

'Reckon it is.' The marshal's tone came with defeat, and maybe a measure of shame. Had Josh's head not been ringing with thunder it might have been encouraging.

'Just don't get too full of yourself, lawdog,' Brint said, gaze still locked with the marshal's. 'No matter what we do our pa will back us up and if it comes down to it he'll make an example out of anyone in front of the whole goddamned town to make sure they don't get highfalutin' notions. You best keep that in mind. Paid-for lawmen ain't a rarity in these parts, neither.' With that, Brint jostled the marshal's shoulder with his own and walked away. Billy let out a chuckle, glanced at Melissa with a grin and started after his brother.

The marshal watched them go until they were out of sight, then turned and glanced at Melissa.

'You awright, miss?' he asked.

She nodded, and a tear slipped down her cheek.

The lawdog stepped off the board-walk and went to the trough, extended a hand. Josh grabbed the man's forearm and the marshal hauled him up out of the trough. Water streamed from his clothing and face and his legs threatened to desert him. He took shallow breaths, each paining his ribs.

'We best get you to the doc's, I reckon,' the marshal said. With a wave of his hand, he stepped back on to the boardwalk. 'Follow me.'

★ ★ ★

'He'll live,' Doc Cranston said, casting a look at Marshal Barsten, who stood, arms folded, leaning against the wall in the small examination room. 'That's more than I can say for some of the poor souls the brothers get hold of.'

Josh sat on the edge of the examination table and Melissa stood near the opposite wall, worry in her blue eyes.

The marshal nodded. 'Reckon that's enough said, Doc.'

Josh's gaze went from the marshal to the doctor, whose wrinkled face held disgust. Here was a man who didn't much appreciate being lorded over, in Josh's estimation, but swallowed it because he was forced to.

Josh had been lucky; no broken ribs and while his jaw would be sore for a few days it hadn't fractured. He reckoned he'd be coughing up trough water for a spell, but if that was the worst of it he couldn't complain.

'Ain't never been hit that hard,' he said, fingers going to his jaw, which had swollen and was already livid with a bruise. His lips were puffy, split.

'Some kind of metal,' Melissa said, speaking for the first time since the attack. 'Across his knuckles. Looked like iron, maybe.'

'Brass,' the marshal said, nodding. 'Brint wasn't taking any chances with you, Mr Dellin. Reckon he recognized you.'

'I take it you know who I am, too?'

The marshal shrugged. 'Your likeness has been in the papers enough, I reckon. You got yourself a reputation. Couple of dime novels about your adventures, I hear tell. You picked the wrong town to ride into, being the sort you are.'

Josh's gaze locked with the lawdog's. 'I want you to arrest those two, Marshal. The third brother, too.'

The marshal's eyebrow cocked. 'For fightin'? Won't do no good, not in this town. 'Sides, Marcus wasn't even there. Can't bring him in for being related.'

'It ain't fightin' I want them arrested for — it's murder.'

'Murder?' The marshal shifted feet, apprehension coming into his eyes. Josh studied the man, seeing someone who had been beaten down, but who might have believed in something once. 'You look plenty living to me, Mr Dellin.'

'There's a young woman at the funeral man's who ain't in such a condition, Marshal. The Chulos are responsible for her death.'

'You got proof of this?' A look of nascent panic came into the man's dull green eyes at the thought of having to bring in any member of the Chulo family.

'I got a witness.' He ducked his chin at Melissa.

The marshal peered at her. 'You saw them kill this woman?'

'No. But I saw them kidnap her after they raped some of the women in my town and I saw them kill a man there.'

'So you saw them take her, but not actually kill her . . . ' The marshal's voice drifted. He was searching for any excuse to avoid bringing in the Chulos and Josh knew it. 'Why didn't you help your friend while he was gettin' his britches kicked all to hell?'

'You saw the whole thing?' Melissa asked.

'I did, from down the street. Saw you didn't make a move even to yell out.'

Josh's brow furrowed. The marshal was placing his own inadequacy on the girl and it was obvious. Josh knew damn well why Melissa hadn't been able to make a move: years of her town leaders drumming non-violence into her brain had paralyzed her.

'I might ask you the same question, Marshal,' Josh said. 'You could have stepped in earlier, if you were watching.

Why didn't you?'

The marshal shifted feet again and swallowed, caught in his own accusation. The answer was just as obvious and it had nothing to do with non-violence. He had been afraid to act, until it looked like it was about to go too far, and had then stepped in only because Miguel Chulo would have wanted it that way.

The doctor let out a small scoff and shook his head, lips pressed tight in a frown. 'Wastin' your breath, Mr Dellin,' he said.

After a moment of tense silence, the marshal turned his gaze back to Josh. 'I can't arrest those men for something no one saw. They might have left that girl on her own, then some bandit came along and killed her, for all I know.'

Josh shook his head, sighed. 'And the man Melissa saw them kill?'

He shrugged. 'That's up to the law in — what town was it you hail from, miss?' He glanced at the girl.

'Thanody.'

The marshal let out a thin humorless laugh. 'That about settles that, then, don't it?' He turned toward the door, shoving his hat back on his head.

'Marshal,' Josh said, stopping him.

The marshal looked back at Josh over his shoulder. 'Yeah, Mr Dellin?'

'You know damn well what those boys are capable of. I suggest you go over to the funeral man's and see for yourself. Maybe after that you won't be so ready to make excuses for them.'

'Reckon I don't have to make excuses for them, Mr Dellin. Their pa's right good at that and if you know anything about him you know the word of your witness won't do a damn bit of good in any court in these parts . . . assuming she lives long enough to testify.'

'I aim to bring those men to justice, Marshal. With your help or without.'

The marshal's gaze saddened as it locked with Josh's. 'Oh, Mr Dellin, that's damn poor judgment on your part, believe me. No matter what reputation you got, Miguel Chulo's got a bigger one in this area. A more powerful one.'

Josh frowned. 'Don't doubt that, but difference between you and me is I ain't afraid of a reputation.'

The marshal laughed. 'No, difference between you and me is you're a fool . . . '

★ ★ ★

After Marshal Barsten left the doctor's office, he paused outside on the boardwalk, a sigh rattling his entire frame. Christ, he was tired. Tired of Miguel Chulo and his rule over this town, tired of the boys and their thinkin' they could just do whatever the hell they wanted to do when they wanted to do it.

He knew in his soul the manhunter and that girl were right: the Chulo boys had committed murder and it wasn't the first time, nor was it likely to be the last. But their deeds, mostly, didn't happen in Coyote Creek, did they?

They happened in other towns. What business of it was his, then, to get involved? What could he do, anyway?

He'd long ago surrendered his claim to righteousness, had the moment he'd first bowed to Miguel's will and accepted money to look the other way on some store owner Chulo planned to shut down illegally.

But that had been a lifetime ago, when he was stronger, able to withstand the guilt. Too many pieces of his soul had flaked off in the intervening years and too many sleepless nights had plagued him, thinking about the unknown victims whose blood stained his hands as much as it did the Chulos'.

He started along the boardwalk, sighing again, his soul dragging behind him. 'Christ, you know you can't do anything about it,' he whispered. That fool manhunter and his highfaluting notions. Judas Priest, he'd find out soon enough you didn't buck the Chulos, not in this town, not in this territory. Miguel had too many connections; the law couldn't touch him.

You recollect the days you used to believe in something? he asked himself, maybe for the millionth time since he'd first caved to Chulo's bribe.

He's been a decent lawman once. He'd carried his pride like his badge, shiny and pinned to his heart. Foolish youth, he told himself. Foolish youth and stupidity. The world didn't hold a place for such naïvety anymore. Now it was survive and watch your own ass and that was that.

He stopped, realizing he had reached the funeral man's place. He reached for the doorhandle, paused, hand gripping the knob.

What good is seeing that girl going to do? he asked himself. None. None whatsoever.

But he was going to do it, anyway, because by some small measure guilt made him feel still human.

He entered the shop, the scents of newly sawn wood filling his nostrils. He went down the aisle lined with cabinets and coffins to the back, then stepped through a curtain. A man looked up from behind a small desk to the left.

'Afternoon, Jebediah,' the marshal said, voice flat as his gaze went to the sheet-covered body lying on the table in the center of the room.

'Marshal,' the smallish man said, nodding. 'You ain't bringing me more work, I hope. Got enough with that — ' He ducked his chin at the table.

'No, the boys been relatively quiet since they rode in. Came to take a look at the girl.'

Jebediah Thatch nodded again, went back to a newspaper he'd been reading.

The marshal went to the body, his hand pausing as it started toward the sheet, then going forward again. He pulled the sheet back, and nausea surged into his belly. With a quick motion he covered the girl and tried to regain control of his composure. Weakness washed through his legs and he swallowed hard.

'Not too damned pretty, is it,

Marshal?' Thatch said, glancing at him.

'No, it goddamned ain't.'

'Them boys been at it again? That's what that manhunter fella seemed to think.'

Legs trembling, the marshal went toward the curtain, wishing to hell he hadn't forced himself to come here. 'Reckon they're always at it. Reckon they might never stop.'

6

The first three hotels Josh and Melissa visited refused to rent rooms to them and Josh was already fed up with it. The proprietors had witnessed the fight in the street and concluded it would be in their best interest to avoid strangers already on the Chulos' bad side.

As he entered the fourth hostelry, his ribs and jaw still aching from the beating, his attitude in even worse shape, he concluded this would be the last stop; if this hotel wouldn't provide rooms he'd set up camp outside of town.

After leaving the doc's, he'd boarded their horses at the livery stable, the livery man being more amenable to the fistful of greenbacks Josh had pulled out of his pocket than the three hotel owners.

Melissa had remained silent the

entire time, and guilt stained her blue eyes. She blamed herself for not helping him against Brint and Billy Chulo; that much was obvious.

'You couldn't have done anything against those two, even if you had tried,' he said as they entered the hotel.

She frowned. 'Couldn't I have? I let them just . . . beat you. I would have let him rape me. What does that say about me?'

'You spent years listening to your leaders' notions; they're ingrained. Not gonna be easy changing them, if that's what you want to do.'

'They could have killed you. And what they did to Tilly Mathews — '

'But they didn't kill me. Men like that, they get cocky, think the world can't touch them. Damn sure they know who I am and wanted to show me who owns this town. Let's hope it's a mistake I can capitalize on.'

She nodded, but tears shimmered in her eyes. She didn't accept his words fully, but he wagered she would dwell on them for a spell and come to see he was right. Yet a measure of worry that she might not be able to act even to save her own life if one of those brothers attacked her simmered in the back of his mind.

The hotel lobby was simple, furnished with worn furniture and a dusty chandelier. A counter, behind which were pigeonholes built into the wall for messages or keys, ran along the west wall and a stairway and mezzanine occupied the north side of the room. They crossed the threadbare carpet to the counter and Josh knew from the look on the face of the small man behind the counter he was in for another argument.

'Please,' the man said, gazing up from beneath a green visor, 'just go somewhere else.' The man was older than Josh by a good ten years but premature lines set deep around his eyes and mouth and early-silvered hair made him look older by twenty.

Josh lightly thumped the heel of his

hand on the counter. 'We've been everywhere else, fella, and I got me a powerful headache out of it.'

The man looked over Josh's battered face. 'I saw what they did to you earlier. It don't pay to go against any of the Chulos. Reckon you found that out firsthand.'

Josh scoffed. 'Reckon they aren't right pleased with the notion I'm here to bring them in for murder.'

Shock jumped on to the hotel man's features and a shudder rattled his bony frame.

'You can't be serious? No one on God's green's gonna take them in for their crimes. You'll just end up like any others who've tried.'

Josh cocked an eyebrow. 'And how's that?'

The hotel man shuddered again. 'Dead, sir. Dead as dead can be. You best take the young lady here and ride on back to wherever you come from, 'fore it's too late.'

'You're starting to sound like a bad

pulp novel, mister.'

'Ain't no better way to put it. I don't like what they've done to this town, but I got a family and a hankering to go on living my life, such as it is.'

'In captivity?'

'I don't call it that.'

'That's about what it amounts to, ain't it?'

'Please, just go back where you came.' The little man's eyes turned pleading.

Josh sighed, leaned his forearms on the counter top. 'You see, I can't do that, mister, 'cause where I came from the Chulos already visited. They kidnapped a young woman, then murdered her. Raped her and left her impaled on a tree a ways outside of town. They raped a number of others in Thanody, too, and killed a fella there in cold blood.'

The little man's face washed shades paler, and the look in his eyes said he did not question Josh's words. 'What do you want from me, sir? I'm just one man. I don't even own a gun.'

Josh straightened and his hand went to the empty holster at his hip. 'Seems I don't at the moment, either, but you'd be surprised what one man can do once he puts his mind to it.'

'One man can get hisself buried right easy, too.'

'Two rooms.' Josh pulled a roll of greenbacks from his pocket. 'How much is it going to take?'

'It ain't about the money.'

'Reckon I'm aware of that, but I'm tellin' you straight, I'm takin' down those men one way or the other, even if I have to camp on Miguel Chulo's doorstep.'

The hotel man's gaze riveted on the counter top for a dragging moment, then with a heavy sigh he turned a register book around and slid it towards Josh. 'They ask, I don't know who the hell you are, didn't see nothin' and didn't know no better.'

'Much obliged.' Josh tossed a couple of bills on to the counter, then peeled off another few and kept them in his hand while he returned the roll to his pocket. 'Enough folks took a stand against them this way, you might get your town back.'

The little man uttered a humorless chuckle. 'We'd all get ourselves buried, mister. That's all we'd do.' He reached behind him and pulled two keys from cubbies. 'Rooms 5 and 6, up the stairs to the right.'

Josh tipped a finger to his hat, took one key and handed the other to Melissa. 'Saw a dress shop down the street a ways when we came in. Way you're dressed, reckon it's bound to attract even more attention. Might be wise to get yourself some regular clothes.' He handed her the other bills he'd saved out and she accepted them, stared at them in her hand.

'Where are you going?' she asked, not looking at him.

'Gonna have me a look around the Chulo place, see what exactly I'm up against.'

A groan came from the hotel man and Josh peered at him.

'Where is it?' Josh asked.

'You have a death wish, don't you, sir?'

'I got a justice wish. Now where is this place?'

'Ride north out of town. You can't miss it.'

Josh nodded, then pushed himself away from the counter, leaving Melissa staring after him as he left the hotel.

* * *

The hotel man was right: you couldn't miss the Chulo mansion. A marvel of Eastern architecture, it was built in an asymmetrical style Josh didn't know the name for and sported a steep multi-gabled roof, shiplap siding and latticework, cut-outs and rows of spindles and knobs. All he knew was it was huge, sprawling, with a veranda that ran the length of the front; afternoon sunlight glinted from spotless multipaned windows. The

107

grounds, manicured and embellished with bright spring flowers, spread out seemingly endlessly, peppered with various outbuildings such as an icehouse and a carriage house, and surrounded by a fancy ten-foot-high iron fence with a double gate at the front.

'Jesus,' Josh whispered, a quiver of trepidation washing over him. Josh didn't quite know what he had expected but the sight of the place was momentarily breathtaking. Apparently sin had paid high rewards for Miguel Chulo.

One thing was certain, Josh wasn't just going to walk in and ask Miguel Chulo to hand over his boys. While he saw no guards, a man of power wasn't likely to be without protection and just because he didn't spot them didn't mean they weren't there. It simply meant they were experts at their job. Given time he might have ferreted them out but since he was at present an open target he'd forgo the bit of reconnaissance. The place told him all he needed to know — Miguel Chulo and his boys had sanctuary here and Josh needed an alternative plan if he expected to bring the killers to justice. Possibly a few would pose as servants, too.

Josh angled his horse about the outside of the south side of the fence, keeping close to the forest that edged the perimeter. His gaze narrowed beneath his Stetson and a sigh trickled from his lips.

He would need to isolate them, he reckoned, one by one. And he would need to do it while avoiding the father.

But how do you get them alone? And in succession, so the ones remaining free didn't go running back to their father and complicate matters?

Men like the Chulo boys likely would be vulnerable in two ways — women and drink. Three, if you added arrogance. If he could take advantage of that, he and Melissa had a chance of coming out of this alive and making a case in some county where Miguel Chulo's influence wasn't so strong.

A tremor of worry went through him

and he reckoned that was a new emotion. He'd never really experienced much in the way of fear before, but a twinge of it took him now. But the fear didn't come for himself. If he died on a job, then so be it. He'd accepted that possibility, even likelihood, years ago. But something was changing inside him, even more so than the notions of black and white he'd clung to for so long before accepting this case.

And that something came with a name: Melissa. Something about the young woman made him think things he had no call thinking. Damned if she wasn't the loveliest thing he'd ever laid eyes on. And damned if he didn't feel a peculiar connection to her right from the start, when she'd stood up to Herridge. He sensed loneliness in her, a longing for something she'd never had, and in a way that made her a reflection of himself, bonded them . . .

Jesus! he chided himself. This was no time to go gettin' himself sweet on some woman he'd only known a short time. What the devil was the matter with him?

A scritching sound cut off any chance of an answer and he cursed himself for losing his focus for the second time since arriving in Coyote Creek.

'Put your hands where I can see 'em, Dellin,' came a voice behind him. Josh raised his hands, tensed for the shot he expected to come.

A man on a horse angled around beside him. The man held a Smith & Wesson on him and his Mex features carried a smug expression.

Marcus Chulo, if Josh figured it right. He looked much like his brothers, slightly older, but something in his scuffed-brown eyes hinted that he just might be the worst of the lot.

'You know me?' Josh asked, keeping his voice steady, refusing to show any intimidation.

The eldest Chulo brother laughed. 'Oh hell, yes. You got your mug in enough papers, don't you? Famous manhunter — men such as myself pay attention to faces we might someday find sniffin' our ass. We saw you ride in earlier. I rode out to tell my father about your arrival while my brothers stayed behind to keep an eye on you and that woman you brought with you from Thanody. I figure my father might want a word with you, otherwise I'd kill you where you sit and be done with it.'

'Reckon I should thank your pa, then.'

Marcus Chulo uttered another laugh, this one full of contempt. 'I reckon you won't feel the same after you talk to him. He's still stuck in Old Mex sometimes, Dellin. Old ones got their ways. They like to intimidate fellows into doing their bidding, control them. Me, I prefer 'em dead.'

'Like that girl we found impaled on the tree a few miles outside of town?' Josh's eyes narrowed, hate bleeding into them. The eldest Chulo's face turned serious. Marcus Chulo might be any number of things but he recognized a threat when confronted with it.

'Don't know what you're talkin' about, manhunter. What girl might that be?'

Josh locked gazes with Marcus Chulo. 'Let's get one thing straight, Chulo. I'm here to bring you in, one way or the other. You're responsible for killing that girl and likely too many others to put a number to.'

'That so? You just expect I'll go with you peaceably, or that my father will turn us all over to you so you can put a bullet in our brains or stretch our necks — that's what you do to most of the men you track down, or isn't that pulp novel accurate?'

'Accurate enough.'

'Get going,' Marcus motioned with his gun, indicating for Josh to ride toward the front of the fence. Josh complied, grasping the reins and angling his horse in a slow walk toward the gate. When they reached it, Marcus motioned for Josh to dismount and open the double iron doors, then climb back on to his horse and continue toward the house.

When they reached the mansion, he dismounted again, Marcus Chulo keeping the gun trained on him the entire time. The eldest brother climbed down slowly, gaze never wavering from Josh, and motioned for him to take the steps and cross the porch.

'Knock,' Marcus ordered and Josh grasped the gold-plated knocker, and banged it against the fortresslike door.

The door opened and a man in a servant's uniform stood there, his features hard, weathered, not the face of a manservant, but that of a hired gun.

The man stepped aside after noticing Marcus behind Josh and allowed them to enter.

The mansion's interior proved as elegant as the exterior had proved large. A great anteroom held polished marble flooring, a crystal chandelier that sparkled as if it contained diamonds. A huge stairway with polished banisters wound to an upper open hallway.

Marcus led Josh to a room to the left, a huge drawing room filled with rich mahogany tables and furniture sporting intricate scrollwork and ball-and-claw feet. A grand piano trimmed in gilt sat in the east corner of the room and a mahogany bar upon which rested crystal decanters on silver plates occupied the west end. Beside the bar stood a man in traditional Mexican clothing, a short gold-braided coat, boiled embroidered shirt and high black boots. The man held a glass half full of amber liquid in one hand and a cigar in the other. His dark face pinpointed his Mex heritage, and his black hair was just starting to gray at the temples. A thin mustache lined his upper lip and his dark eyes reflected a meanness that might have even surpassed the cruelty in Marcus's devil eyes.

'Good afternoon — Mr Dellin, is it?' His voice carried an accent, something the Chulo boys didn't share. Josh reckoned the boys had been raised in the States. He also guessed from their lighter skin that Miguel Chulo had married a white woman.

Josh gave him a slight nod. 'Wish I could say it was a pleasure.'

Miguel Chulo's dark eyes settled on Josh, arrogance and a smug superiority coming into them. 'It is proper to remove your hat when in a man's home, Mr Dellin.'

Marcus Chulo laughed and suddenly knocked Josh's hat from his head. It landed on the floor and Josh was barely able to restrain the urge to spin on the boy and knock the smile off his lips. But the move would have been suicide and right now he didn't know where this meeting was leading. He'd made a damn fool mistake getting himself into this position, and getting out of it alive to mount a counter attack was his priority now.

Marcus Chulo backed up to the door, leaned a shoulder against the jamb.

'Found him wandering outside the compound,' Marcus said.

The senior Chulo nodded. 'Forgive me if I don't offer you any, eh?' He smiled and took a swig of his drink, finishing it, then set the glass on the bartop. 'To what do I owe the displeasure of this visit, then, Mr Dellin?'

Josh folded his arms, locked gazes with the man. 'Had a run-in with your boys in town, Chulo. They got something that don't belong to them. My gun. I came to get it back.'

'Did you, now?' Miguel Chulo took a puff from his cigar. 'I've been in my line of business a long time, Mr Dellin. I've met with your country's leaders, local and state, and others from countries as far away as Spain. I pride myself on my ability to recognize a liar.'

Marcus let out a laugh. 'He said he intends to bring us in for murder.'

Miguel's eyebrow arched and dark lights twinkled in his eyes. 'Murder, Mr Dellin? You have proof of that?'

Josh remained quiet. He had no desire to tell the elder Chulo about his witness.

Marcus saved him the trouble. 'Reckon he thinks he's got a witness. Some Thanotite he drug with him all the way to Coyote Creek.'

'Is that true, Mr Dellin?' Miguel studied Josh, who still remained silent. 'Ah, no need to answer. I see it in your eyes. But I am sure you are well aware that no one, especially in this part of the territory, takes those people with any seriousness? Yes?'

Josh's expression didn't change. 'I take it serious; that's all you need to know.'

The man's face tightened, anger glittering in his dark eyes. 'I can see from the bruises on your face, Mr Dellin, you have met my other sons, no? Do not be so foolish as to remain in town and meet them again. The results could be much worse, especially for the young woman.'

A spike of fury pierced Josh's belly. 'Getting right down to the threats, Chulo? Let me give you one in return: anything happens to that young woman and there won't be a judge or bought-off lawman in the territory who'll be able to save your neck from gettin' stretched. I make myself clear?'

Marcus Chulo suddenly stepped up behind him and the cold barrel of the Smith & Wesson jabbed into Josh's neck.

Miguel held up his hand, but his face had reddened. He wasn't a man used to threats or challenges to his word.

'Best let me kill him now,' Marcus said. 'No use chancin' him comin' back on us.'

'Not in my home, Marcus, not on my doorstep.'

'We could say he busted in here, tried to kill — '

'No! I said.' Miguel Chulo's face went from red to purple. It was plain he brooked no argument from his sons and no challenge to his authority.

Josh stooped, picked up his hat and set it on his head. He turned, brushed past Marcus Chulo, giving him a smug smile. 'I'll see you again, Marcus, and you'll be beggin' for your life the way I reckon that young woman must have begged for hers.'

Marcus looked ready to pull the trigger but a glance at his father prevented him from doing so.

'Leave this town, Mr Dellin,' came Miguel Chulo's voice behind Josh as he went toward the drawing room doors. 'I won't tell you again. By sundown. Or I'll let my boys use their judgment.'

Josh looked back to Miguel Chulo. 'Wasn't aware they had a lick of any.' He walked from the room and toward the front door, fighting to keep his legs from shaking and hold on to an aura of confidence he reckoned he didn't truly have.

Fact was, he was damned lucky to be walking out of this alive and the next time that luck might run out.

7

Melissa Gatner stayed in her room for a half hour after Josh Dellin left to go scout out the Chulo grounds. Sitting on the edge of the bed in the small room that contained only a bed, a dresser with a porcelain wash basin and pitcher, a night table and a hard-backed chair, myriad thoughts rushed through her mind.

She found herself more than slightly worried about Josh Dellin riding out to the Chulo place alone. She had seen what those men could do, after all, how they had killed one of the town leaders in cold blood, what they had done to that poor girl they'd carried off. If they caught Josh looking around, he might get more than a beating this time.

She shouldn't have been having these feelings for a man she barely knew, she told herself. Not this soon. But there was something about him, something in his eyes. She saw loneliness there, but also kindness, a strength of character she had never glimpsed in any of the men in Thanody. The men in her town chose women the way they chose livestock, and with an eye toward furthering their line and their personal pleasure. That fact had only become more clear to her since meeting Josh Dellin.

Things weren't as black and white as Thanody's leaders made them out to be, were they? They never had been, but she had turned a deaf ear to the voice inside her soul that had told her so, warned her; and had turned a blind eye to the sights of their harsh punishments and words. Women meant nothing to them; in the end that had led to two young women's horrible deaths, Tilly's and Martha's.

She stood, sweat trickling from beneath her arms and between her ample breasts. The room was stifling, so she went to the window and raised it, though it helped little because of the heavy wool clothing she wore. She peered out into the street, for a moment watching some of the townswomen stroll along the boardwalks. A curious fear played on their faces, one she recognized, one that came with domination. These people were afraid of the Chulos, resented their rule but dared do nothing about it. She could well identify with that feeling.

But in another way they possessed a liberty she did not enjoy in Thanody — the freedom to walk about dressed as they saw fit. She also saw the casual smiles women gave menfolk as they passed. No man in Thanody would ever tolerate such from a woman. Women there were not allowed to look directly at men; they were ordered to look at the ground, speak softly and respectfully. Even during procreation, which came with a blanket sandwiched between them with a small square cut into the fabric, a woman was forbidden to open her eyes. They were not allowed to touch, to embrace or simply feel safe in their lover's arms. Relations between a man and a woman were only performed out of necessity, breeding. She doubted any man in Thanody was capable of such a blasphemous emotion as love.

Thanody was a dying town, she had begun to think. Dying by its own stubborn resolve in clinging to antiquated views and policies set down by domineering men, and old values and proclamations that had never been intended to be corrupted the way they'd come to be. The sect's forefathers had been stern, righteous men, who'd suffered much from violence and persecution, and likely they'd had their reasons for laying down such stringent rules. But things had changed over the years; those rules had become twisted by men more concerned with domination and cowardice than truth and survival.

She had known it all along; many of the women knew it as well, though they would never admit to such. Her short time with Josh Dellin had convinced her of that more than ever.

She pondered the feelings blossoming for him inside her soul. They were unlike anything she'd felt previously. Warmth, deep glowing warmth, like the first breath of spring, the opening of a wildwood flower. With that feeling came curious desires, stirrings. She wanted to be near him, perhaps even craved to be, and perhaps even longed to feel her lips and body against —

No! Such things were not permissible for a young woman to entertain. She could not possibly be falling in love with a man she had just met. She did not even know what love was, if it even existed. It was merely her loneliness overwhelming her, clouding her emotions and thoughts.

Her hand went to the bosom of her wool dress and she let out a small sigh. He had given her the money for new clothing but she was strangely frightened of using it. Not that he expected anything for his generous gift — he did not, and that was plain. He was a good man, though one who lived by a strange code of violence she didn't understand.

No, her fear came from changing a lifetime of habit, of order, of ingrained belief.

'There is nothing to be frightened of,' she whispered. 'You cannot return to Thanody anyway. How you dress no longer matters . . . '

It never really had, she realized. The drab clothing was nothing more than a symbol, no, a *brand* placed upon the women of the town by those who wished to make their absolute rule known.

A tear slipped from her eye, and she quickly brushed it away. Why was everything so difficult now? Why was change, even when wanted, so terribly frightening? Why were her thoughts so very confused?

You're falling in love with him . . .

That's not possible, another voice within countered.

But did a woman really need a given

period of time to see into another's soul and know, just know, that this man was the one she could give her life to?

No, not give her life to, but share it with. Wasn't that the way things should be? To live not as a possession but as a true and equal partner?

Oh, how the Thanody leaders would scoff at that. They considered such thinking dangerous, worthy of punishment. Men who didn't believe in violence, but behind closed doors were quick with a switch on their women's backsides.

They were cowards; Josh was right. They could privately harm, while publicly proclaiming such foul acts of violence were the Devil's tool. Their lofty edicts were nothing more than a pitiful excuse for them to back away from those more powerful than they, and conduct their lives in the controlled fantasy they had created.

She let out a small laugh. The truth of it. The truth she'd too long ignored.

But no longer. She could choose now

to be different. She could choose to live.

Could Josh Dellin ever find it within himself to love a woman like her? A woman at whom school children had made cow and pig sounds whenever she walked past, a woman who men in her town looked upon with disdain and even disgust? A woman destined to live out a life in subservience to old men too blind and unfeeling to care?

Years of conditioning told her no, he never would. But a glimmer of something she had seen in his eyes told her perhaps a spark of hope existed he could love her in return.

But not dressed like a spinster. A woman too frightened to shuck the trappings of her repressive life. Her fingers went to the ties of her bonnet and, fingers shaking and head lifting, she pulled at the strings. She hesitated, then with a quick breath yanked the bonnet loose and tossed it backwards on to the bed. Her strawberry blonde hair cascaded over her shoulders and framed her cherubic face. She ran her fingers through her hair, fluffing it.

The first step, she told herself. The first step to freedom, no matter what terrors the future held.

Steeling herself with a deep breath, she went to the door, opened it and stepped out into the hallway.

Minutes later, she left the hotel and headed down the boardwalk, sunlight warm on her face and shining from her hair. The breeze stirred the strands, a sensation she was unused to. She couldn't recollect a time she'd been in public without her bonnet. She forced her gaze to remain level, her head high. Men gave her smiles as they passed. She struggled to smile back, but the expression came hard. It would take time. But she would learn.

The dress shop was a few blocks down and by the time she reached it she was perspiring even more.

When she entered the dress shop a small bell above the door announced her arrival and an older woman greeted her. The woman looked her up and down, smiled.

'You realize how hot it is out there to be walkin' around in that dress?' the old woman asked.

Melissa nodded. 'I came for lighter clothing.' How did one ask for women's things? She'd never had to do that, had never even thought about such a thing. 'The women in my town wear only these dresses.'

The old woman cocked an eyebrow. 'Lordy, what town might that be?'

'Thanody.' She was almost embarrassed to say it.

The older woman placed a bony hand on her shoulder and nodded. 'I heared the menfolk there got it right fine for themselves.'

Melissa's smile came naturally, unbidden. 'I reckon you might be right.'

'Well, come on, let's fetch you something you won't cook in.'

Half an hour later Melissa left the shop wearing a blue gingham dress that hugged the plump curves of her body. A shiver of trepidation washed through her as she stepped out on to the boardwalk and her cheeks flushed with crimson. She felt almost naked somehow, but also unburdened in a way she could not have explained. She peered down at her full bosom and rounded hips and maybe for the first time she actually saw herself as a woman instead of the lonely waste of flesh the menfolk in Thanody proclaimed her to be.

A few minutes later she stopped at another small shop and with the money she had left over from the dress she selected a bottle of perfume that tickled her nostrils when she sniffed it. It was a light flowery scent, like midnight jasmine, and she dabbed a bit behind her ears and at her throat as she stepped back outside into the late afternoon.

Maybe she was fooling herself. Maybe no matter how much she tried to pretty herself up she was still the same useless cow folks told her she was. But for at least a short spell, she was willing to believe otherwise. Even if it was only a delusion.

'Well, my — my, you pretty up right nice, don't you, Bessie?'

The voice jerked her from her thoughts, froze her where she stood on the boardwalk. Fear shivered through her. Leaning against a supporting beam was one of the men who'd killed Tilly. The one who'd taken Josh's gun, the one called Brint.

'Leave me be,' was all she managed to get out, her voice trembling.

Brint laughed, pushed himself away from the beam. 'Now, why would I want to go and do a thing like that? Fact is, I like my women on the plump side, Bessie. More cushion for the ride, you get my meanin'.'

Heat washed into her cheeks. 'Don't call me that.'

''Case you haven't figured it out yet, Bessie, this here is my town and I can do whatever ta hell I damn well want.'

'You murdered that girl.' She tried to put conviction and courage in her voice, but her words came barely audible. She wanted to scream, run, but there was nowhere to go. No one in this town would likely help her and Josh was still out surveying the Chulo place.

'Reckon that's something that'll never be proved nor cared about.' Brint's eyes narrowed and dark lights glittered within them. Another shiver went through her.

He grabbed her arm, his fingers gouging in. She let out a small sound, but fright suffocated any scream she might have unleashed. The perfume bottle dropped from her hand and thudded on the boardwalk.

He dragged her along, her legs nearly collapsing beneath her, then pulled her off the boardwalk and into an alley running beside a saloon. Her heart pounded and her pulse throbbed in her ears and throat, and she wondered if she just wouldn't faint before he took her.

'Please,' she whispered as he jammed her against a wall. His groping hands explored her breasts and drifted lower.

'You can beg all you want, Bessie, but take my word for it when I tell ya I ain't got a goddamn ounce of compassion or conscience. This is gonna happen and whether you like it or not doesn't matter a goddamn to me. Reckon all I got to worry about is where I'm gonna hide your body.'

Tears flooded her eyes, streamed down her face as he jammed his lips against hers. She could taste the rancid flavor of old bacon and whiskey, rotting teeth. He laid a smear of saliva across her cheek and his hand found her thigh, fingers groping.

And still she could not resist. Could not fight back. If she just lifted her knee, buried it in his middle parts, she might be able to run, get away. But where could she run to? She'd ridden into the lion's den with Josh without the thought she perhaps should have given it. She'd placed herself in a position to be the victim of a man, the way she always had.

It's not your fault . . . a voice thin

and fragile came from somewhere inside her.

But that voice didn't matter because Brint Chulo was going to rape and kill her and any chance she might have had at freedom was now a mocking epitaph.

8

Josh Dellin boarded his roan at the livery and headed back to the hotel, disgusted with himself at having been caught by one of the Chulo brothers but relieved that he was still alive to be able to be disgusted with himself.

'You're getting downright sloppy,' he chastised himself, a frown creasing his lips as he strode along the boardwalk. A week ago he wouldn't have allowed himself to have been so distracted, but now everything seemed to be coming to a head inside him. His time as a manhunter might well have passed and he had to admit that to himself. His viewpoint had been changing, subtly, for a spell, but certainly nevertheless, much the way Tredder's position had. Trouble was, he'd accepted what looked to be not only the most difficult but the most dangerous case of his career, so it was a damn inconvenient time to deal with distraction.

It was the type of thing that got manhunters killed and he wasn't ready to have 'shot while lost in thought' chiseled on his gravestone.

He couldn't afford another mistake. He needed to focus on isolating the Chulo boys, which was going to be a damn sight harder now that he'd directly informed Miguel Chulo of his intentions.

That wasn't the goddamned brightest notion you've ever had, he told himself, but the man's attitude had rankled him. He had never cottoned to arrogant types who thought themselves above others, and Miguel Chulo ranked with the worst of the breed. He knew what his sons were doing, yet still covered it up for them. He was no better than they, if more refined.

A killer was still a killer, he reckoned, even if he was gold-plated.

And that being the case, he now had to deal quickly with Miguel Chulo's threat to get out of Coyote Creek because Melissa's life was in imminent danger.

He entered the hotel, crossed the lobby to the stairs. Muscles balled to either side of his jaw, the more he dwelled on Miguel Chulo's threat toward the girl.

You're letting your emotions get in the way. Something about that young woman . . .

Dammit, he should have just left her back in Thanody! What the hell had he been thinkin', anyway? Something about her had immediately clouded his judgment and the more time he spent around her, even though that time could be measured in brief hours, the more he felt inclined to let his thoughts run wild.

What the devil was wrong with him?

He reached his room, entered, then closed the door behind him. Letting out a sigh, he went to the basin and splashed tepid water into his face, then toweled off on his sleeve. He found himself uncertain of his next step. With most of the men he chased it was a simple matter of tracking them down and getting the jump on them, then either bringing them back for hanging or defending himself with his Peacemaker.

In his mind, Josh ran through his brief encounters with the brothers. He pegged Marcus as the most dangerous, with Brint right behind him, though maybe a little more hotheaded and impulsive, judging from the sneak attack earlier. If he had to make a wager, he bet the youngest, Billy, would be the most unstable and green.

But Billy . . . what Melissa had told him about not wanting the women he'd cornered . . .

Where would he go in this town to find that kind of thing? Some saloons catered to that type, in a hushed manner, but which one? Askin' outright would be problematic, either in finding someone with the type of information or in alerting the Chulos he was planning something. But if he could catch Billy drunk . . .

That meant dogging him, somehow, moving on him after dark and being damn careful about it, since he didn't know how many of the townsfolk might go running back to Miguel Chulo.

'Dammit!' He banged a fist against the dresser top, frustration tightening his nerves. He wasn't used to being in this position and it was his own fault. And with Melissa threatened he liked it even less. He needed time and he had damn little.

'You've got to convince her to leave,' he whispered. 'You've got to get her someplace safe first.'

That was the only way to ensure her safety and have her ready to testify if he was able to bring the Chulos in.

He went to the door, opened it, then stepped out into the hallway. Her room was next door. He had a notion persuading her to leave wasn't going to go smoothly, but he had to try.

He banged on her door, waited. No

answer came, so he knocked again. Still no answer.

He suddenly recollected he'd given her money to buy a dress. Had she had gone to the shop? A sudden quiver of dread went through him. When he'd given her the money he'd reckoned she would be safe in broad daylight for the time being, but now, after meeting with Miguel Chulo, that might not be the case. They had checked in over two hours ago, so if she had gone to buy a dress she should have returned by now.

He went downstairs and rang the bell on the counter. The small man came from the back room and the expression on his face said he was none-too-happy to see Josh.

'The young woman I came in with — ' Josh said.

The man nodded. 'She went out over an hour ago. I didn't see her come back.'

'You see any of the Chulo brothers anywhere about?'

'Nope, and I sure hope to hell I don't, neither. But I reckon with you here it's only a matter of time till one of 'em comes traipsin' in here.'

Josh nodded, then turned and went toward the door. Outside, he peered down the boardwalk in the direction of the dress shop but saw no sign of Melissa. He noticed a boy of about twelve staring into an alley halfway between the hotel and the shop and even from the distance the child had a peculiar look on his face, one of fascination mixed with fear.

A leaden sensation hit his belly and he started for the boy. The child noticed him running toward him and immediately lit out down the street, holding a hand to his head so his hat wouldn't fly off. Josh's dread increased and his hand reflexively went for his Peacemaker.

He whispered a curse at finding the holster empty, having forgotten Brint had relieved him of the piece a few hours before.

'Christ — '

As he reached the alley, his manhunter's caution taking over, he pressed himself against the wall of a shop and peered around the corner.

For an instant he froze, the sight in the alley sending a surge of fury through his veins. Brint had Melissa jammed against the wall, his hand groping at her thigh and his mouth pressed against her lips.

Emotion overcame him and he leaped from the boardwalk, charged into the alley. He covered the ground between him and the outlaw in three bounds. Brint turned his face just as Josh reached him.

Josh grabbed two handfuls of the man's shirt, whirled him around. Letting go with one hand, he snapped a short punch into Brint's face. Brint Chulo's nose cracked and blood spurted. He let out a yell and threw a short punch.

Josh ducked, and the punch whipped over his head. He came back up, launching a sharp uppercut that connected with the sound of blocks colliding under Brint's jaw.

Brint's dark eyes washed blank and

he almost went down.

Josh backed off only an instant but his adversary somehow managed to throw a punch even while semi-conscious. And throw it with power. It took Josh flush on the chin, sent an explosion of stars cascading before his eyes.

He shook his head, getting it clear, quickly followed with a right cross to Brint's temple. Brint staggered forward a step and Josh arced another uppercut that lifted him an inch off his feet and sent him reeling backward, to slam into the wall of the saloon.

Josh gave him no time to recover. Fury overwhelming him, he threw three short punches, each snapping Brint's head back against the wall with a loud bang.

Josh stepped back and Brint Chulo pitched forward, blood streaming from his nose and mouth, eyes rolling up. He crashed into the ground, gasping, groaning, struggling to push himself up to hands and knees, but failing.

Josh glanced at Melissa, whose face was a mask of terror and relief at the same time. 'You all right?'

She nodded, tears streaking down her face. 'He was going to — ' her voice trembled.

Josh stepped over to her and drew her close. She pressed her face against his chest and tears soaked his shirt. He held her, while Brint Chulo groaned in the dirt.

After a moment, Josh drew back, then leaned down and yanked his stolen Peacemaker from Brint's belt. Brint's own gun occupied his holster.

'Believe this is mine,' Josh said, holstering the Peacemaker.

He gripped Melissa's arm and began to lead her from the alleyway. He'd inform the marshal of the attack, though he reckoned it wouldn't do a damn bit of good.

A noise from behind reached his ears, a scuffing sound of metal against leather, and ice washed through his belly. He flung Melissa aside, knowing he'd made another misjudgment in thinking Brint Chulo was too beaten to be a threat.

In the same move his hand whipped for his Peacemaker. He'd always been fast. Sometimes his speed got in the way of his accuracy, in fact, and he had to slow himself down. But this time the move came with pure instinct and his hand blurred as it loosed the gun.

In a heartbeat he took in the scene. Chulo had half risen to his feet and was drawing his own gun.

Josh triggered three shots, only one of them hitting the Chulo brother. But that one was enough. It punched into Brint Chulo's chest and kicked him backward, slamming him against the wall, his own gun dangling from his suddenly lifeless fingers. Then the outlaw fell face first to the ground. Dust stirred by his impact settled over him and blood pooled beneath his body, soaking into the dirt.

Melissa's hands went to her mouth and her eyes widened in shock. Josh stared at the brother for a moment, making certain this time he would not be getting up, then holstered his Peacemaker.

'This is going to go over goddamn well with the marshal,' he said, without humor.

★ ★ ★

'Where are we going?' Melissa asked as Josh touched her elbow and guided her down the boardwalk. Already a crowd was gathering before the alley where lay the body of Brint Chulo. Some of the faces held shock, but a good many more held subtle relief and some even a hint of gloating. They were glad to be rid of at least one Chulo, but Josh had no doubt there would be others who ran to Miguel, tried to curry favor by telling him his son had been murdered and who had committed the act.

Josh steered Melissa off the boardwalk and across the street. 'To the livery.'

'Why?' Melissa's face had gone pale, and she was trembling.

'Won't take the marshal long to discover I've killed one of the Chulos. Not sure how he'll react but I got a notion he'll be too afraid to go against Miguel.'

They reached the livery and he guided her inside. The musky aroma of hay, horse dung and old leather assailed his nostrils. The attendant was nowhere to be seen, and he reckoned the man was probably amongst the crowd gathered at the alley.

'We're riding out?' Melissa asked.

He turned to face her, his features grim. 'No, you are. I'm gettin' you some place safe because Miguel threatened you when I talked to him earlier. He'll make good on that threat a hell of a lot faster now that I've killed his son.'

'You talked to him?' Shock widened her eyes.

'Didn't have much choice. Marcus caught me nosin' around the place. My own stupidity nearly got me killed and it's put you in more danger.'

'I'm not leaving you to go after them alone.' Determination and resolve steadied her voice. He wasn't used to arguing with women and he searched for words to persuade her to do just what she was told, but couldn't find any. He couldn't order her like the men in Thanody, so he decided to lay out the truth and hope she went for it.

'Please, Melissa. I'm better workin' this alone. If you stay I'll just end up worrying about you and that will get us both killed, most like.'

'You'd worry about me?' Shock turned to surprise and something else that sent a shiver through his innards.

Heat flushed into his cheeks. 'Already caught myself doin' it, truth to tell.'

'Way you'd worry about any woman you had with you on a case?'

He shifted feet, sighed, looked at the ground. Damn, this was suddenly far more uncomfortable than he had bargained for.

'Never took a woman with me on a

case before, so can't tell you for certain.' He was trying to back-pedal and from the expression in her eyes she knew exactly what he meant.

She suddenly came up on to her toes and kissed him, then just as hurriedly pulled back. He reckoned it was as much a surprise to her as it was to him that she had acted on such an impulse, but maybe being repressed all those years in Thanody had finally become too much.

'I'm sorry,' she whispered, her fingertips going to her lips.

It took him a moment to shake off the spell of how her soft lips had felt on his, their sweet taste, and get his thoughts functioning again.

'Don't be. Another moment and I might have taken the liberty myself.'

'It was so . . . different from the way that brother . . . in the alley, I mean . . .'

'It's meant to be something given not taken, I reckon.'

'I'm not riding out without you. I'm

staying with you, here.' Her voice had become even more resolute.

He had fostered a slim hope she'd see it his way but that hope was now gone and the kiss had put the nail in the coffin.

The point became suddenly moot as a figure appeared in the livery doorway. Marshal Barsten stood there, face strained, hand on the butt of the six-shooter in his holster.

'Someone saw you two come this way,' the lawdog said, voice weary.

Two other figures suddenly came up behind him and he twisted his head to glance at each.

'Arrest that man, Marshal,' insisted the older of the two. Miguel Chulo's eyes glittered with anger. Beside him stood Marcus, who looked a hair's breadth from drawing his gun and shooting.

Josh edged in front of Melissa, using his body as a shield.

'How'd you get here so fast, Miguel?' Barsten asked, sighing. 'I just sent a man out to tell you what happened.'

Miguel shot a hateful glance at Josh. 'I was riding into town with Marcus to discuss this man — ' He ducked his chin at Josh. 'Your rider met us just coming in, and told me what happened. We saw you heading here and followed. I demand this man be arrested and hanged for the murder of my son.'

'Miguel, we don't quite know the story behind it yet. I got folks who might have seen Brint attack this young woman.'

'Folks who will testify to it, Marshal?' The implication in Miguel Chulo's voice was plain.

Barsten's shoulders sagged. 'No . . . I suppose not. But your sons attacked Mr Dellin and this woman here earlier today in plain view of everyone. I saw it myself.'

Miguel's face went red. He plainly didn't appreciate the marshal's backtalk and Josh was frankly surprised the lawdog was even bothering to go through the motions.

'My boys were simply having fun, Barsten. This man had no right to kill Brint in cold blood. Do your job, before I need remind you of the influence I have in this town.'

Josh eyed the senior Chulo. 'That's puttin' it right out there, isn't it, Chulo?'

Miguel Chulo shot him a vicious look but ignored the statement.

'You needn't remind me,' Barsten said, deflating all the way. 'But I need to remind you there could be inquiries if things aren't done proper and we don't know what happened yet.' The marshal caught Josh's gaze, almost pleading with him to tell him something that would give him an out, but knowing that would be impossible.

'I killed him, Marshal,' Josh said, voice steady, keeping an eye on Marcus, hand ready to go for his gun the moment the Chulo boy got stupid and went to draw. 'He was trying to rape this young woman.'

'That is simply preposterous!' Miguel

said, spittle gathering at the corners of his mouth. 'This man threatened me earlier today. You are using a lie as an excuse to gun down my son in cold blood.'

It occurred to Josh that Miguel didn't seem overly grieved at the loss of Brint, more indignant over the fact someone had dared take a step against him, as if it were a personal slight.

'He drew on me,' Josh said. 'I defended myself. And I defended this young woman.'

'Foolishness!' Miguel's face went a shade redder. 'You are nothing more than a hired killer, Mr Dellin. You promised me earlier you would murder my family and now you have taken the first step toward doing so.'

'Reckon I'm not the only one quick with a threat, am I, Mr Chulo?' Josh locked gazes with the magnate. 'Way I recollect, a short time ago you made one toward this young woman.'

'Nonsense. I am a respected businessman. Marshal, I demand this man's arrest, or do I need to contact the governor's office to see it done and that you are removed from your position?'

Barsten sighed heavily again and took a step into the livery. 'I'll need you to come with me, Mr Dellin, least till we straighten out the details.'

'Till he's hangin' from a cottonwood, you mean,' Marcus said, taking a step forward. 'You'll pay for what you done to Brint. You and her both.' Marcus's gaze settled on Melissa and a chill went through Josh.

'Marcus!' snapped Miguel, casting his son an angry glare.

The marshal eyed them both, then Josh and Melissa. 'Ma'am, you going to back up his story about Brint attacking you?'

'That is a matter for a court to decide, Barsten,' said Miguel. 'Do your job.'

'I am doing my job, Mr Chulo. Trying to at any rate.' Something in Barsten's tone said he no longer really knew what his job was and Josh again got the impression of a man who had believed in something once, but had let himself be railroaded for too long and lost sight of his principles.

'I'll testify to everything he said,' Melissa said, stepping out from behind Josh. 'I kept my mouth shut way too long in Thanody. I won't any longer.'

The marshal nodded. 'You'll come with me, Dellin, and we'll set up an inquiry, let the girl testify.' The way the marshal said it plainly showed he didn't hold out much hope for it mattering. 'Meanwhile, young lady, you stay off the street.' The marshal looked at Marcus, whose lips turned with a slight grin. The lawdog hesitated, reading the same thing Josh had read: Marcus was a threat to the young woman.

'Marshal, you can't leave her alone,' Josh said, his heart pounding. He half-considered trying to shoot it out with them, but that would have just gotten Melissa killed all the faster.

'Marshal, do your job,' Miguel said again, the threat heavy in his tone.

The marshal looked at Josh almost apologetically. 'I'll need your gun, Mr Dellin . . . kindly unbuckle your belt and let it fall to the ground.'

Josh's gaze swept to each face, but he saw no choice. He felt like a man walking to the gallows. His fingers pried at his buckle, unfastening it. He let the gunbelt slip to the ground. The marshal drew his own weapon, motioned Josh away from his belt.

'You,' the lawdog said, looking at Melissa. 'Go back to wherever you're staying. Now.'

Melissa looked pleadingly at Josh and he nodded. There was nothing else to do for the moment. He wanted to tell her to ride out as soon as she got the chance, but it would do no good. She wouldn't go and one of the Chulos would only catch her on the way out if she tried.

The young woman walked past Miguel Chulo, dislike on her face. She paused, her gaze not wavering from his. 'Spent my whole life cowering and taking orders from your type, sir. Those days are over. Your sons are vicious killers. They murdered the young girl who's down at the funeral man's. They deserve their punishment, every last one of them. Time was I would have been revolted at seeing a man killed, but I got a notion now I'll only feel relief when the other two of your kin meet their maker.'

'How dare you, a woman, speak to me in such an insolent manner!' Miguel Chulo's hand came up, open-palmed, paused. Fire burned in his eyes.

Melissa stood her ground. 'Go ahead, Mr Chulo. Strike me. Show everybody how much of a man you are!' She stared, body rigid, ready for the blow.

Miguel Chulo's mouth quivered and his jaw muscles knotted. But he lowered his hand. 'Go!' he said, transferring his gaze from her to the marshal.

Melissa walked out of the livery, Marcus appearing to consider going after her but a flashed look from his father told him it wasn't the time. It also said that time would indeed come. Soon.

'Let's go, Mr Dellin,' the marshal said, stooping to retrieve the gunbelt, then slinging it over his shoulder. Josh started out of the livery, pausing to capture Miguel Chulo's gaze.

'I'm tellin' you once again, Chulo. Leave that girl be or I will personally do to you what I did to your son, only a hell of a lot slower . . . '

Miguel Chulo laughed, the arrogance back in his manner. 'You heard him, Marshal, did you not? A clear threat. This man is nothing more than a glorified murderer.'

'Court will determine that, Mr Chulo,' the marshal said, defeat still in his tone.

'It will, indeed,' Miguel said.

That told Josh everything he needed to know about the fairness of trial in Coyote Creek.

9

Dusk filled the marshal's small office with shadows and blood. The setting sun's crimson light stabbed through a small front window, falling in gory slices across the worn wooden floorboards and reaching into the cell, against whose bars Josh Dellin leaned, arms folded, face fraught with tension. Shadows gathered in the corners like mocking black ghosts awaiting an outcome Josh was sure would occur, if it had not already — a young woman's death.

He'd been stuck in the cell for hours, pacing, nerves buzzing, mind racing. He felt screams struggling to burst from his innards, screams of frustration and for the first time in his career terror over the welfare of a young woman. By now Melissa Gatner might be dead. She was alone, vulnerable to Marcus or

Billy Chulo, and that worried him more than his own predicament and whatever mock trial the marshal and Miguel Chulo would convene.

Marshal Barsten had left nearly immediately after locking him in the cell and hadn't returned. Before leaving, the lawdog had shoved Josh's gun into a drawer of his desk, which was too far from the cell to be reached. The door keys hung from a peg on the opposite wall, also too far away for him to have any chance of getting to it.

The memory of Melissa's kiss came to his mind and his fingertips went to his lips. It didn't matter they had known each other for only a short time; he was falling in love with the young woman and if anything had happened to her he would kill all the Chulos, including Miguel, somehow.

The door opened and Josh's gaze jerked to the figure that entered. The marshal closed the door, went to the wall and ignited the lantern, then lit another on the opposite wall, dispelling the shadows. He then went to a small table beneath the window and poured himself coffee from a blue-enameled pot into a tin cup, keeping his back to Josh.

'You might as well quit starin' at me that way,' he said after taking a sip. 'I know damn well what you're thinking.'

'Do you, Marshal?' Josh's hands went to the bars, gripping them hard enough to make the tendons stand out like white snakes.

'You're worried about the young woman. Don't be. She's fine. I made sure she was in her room at the hotel. Wasn't hard to figure out which one. Only one hotel fella I know might be sympathetic to anybody's cause against the Chulos.' The marshal turned toward him, eyes narrowed. 'Reckon Bittner didn't tell you he owned a small cattle business once. Miguel Chulo wanted it, forced Bittner out of business. Bittner never said as much to Chulo, but he damn well held a grudge. But he's scared of Miguel too. Lots of folks in this town are.'

The words brought a measure of relief. At least Melissa was alive . . . for the time being. That meant he still had a chance. 'And Marcus and Billy? Miguel?'

The marshal licked his lips, then stared at his coffee. 'They made arrangements for Brint's funeral, least Miguel and Marcus did. Ain't seen hide of Billy. I saw the both of 'em ride back out towards their homestead.'

'That don't mean one or the other won't circle back.'

The lawman shrugged. 'No, I s'pose it don't, but I can't babysit them every minute of the day. I took a chance just sticking close to them. Miguel ain't too goddamned happy about it, either. I'll hear about it sooner or later, likely sooner, and likely lose my job.' The lawdog paused, sipped at his coffee. 'Thing of it is, I don't even know what's got into me, Mr Dellin. I know better than to buck anything Miguel says. Yet I did. I must be plain tired of livin'.'

'That ain't it, Marshal. Those boys

are killers, and you know it. You still got a conscience in you somewhere. And you know damn well I shot Brint in self-defense. He was going to rape Melissa.'

'Right on Miguel's doorstep? I doubt it.'

'Do you? Maybe those boys wouldn't risk goin' against their father's orders for someone living in Coyote Creek but who'd miss a Thanotite? Who'd be like to notice she was gone or ask after her?'

The marshal sighed, went to his desk and fell heavily into his chair. He clasped his cup in both hands. 'Truth to tell, it don't matter what I know, Mr Dellin. You picked the wrong goddamn town to do what you do and everyone knows that's hired killing. See, I got a notion you ain't the lying type. I reckon you did kill that boy in self-defense, but I also got the notion even if you hadn't at some point you would have killed him in cold blood just for the crimes you say he committed.'

Josh's eyes narrowed. The marshal

was right and he wouldn't deny it. 'You know they call themselves Prairie Wolves?'

The lawdog nodded. 'Heard tell the rumor.'

'They rape women, leave their underthings hanging in trees, like they were pissing on their territory.'

'Heard tell that rumor, too.'

'I've seen it, in Thanody. It's no rumor.'

'Yet, for the sake of argument, Mr Dellin, not a soul in Thanody will testify to that fact. Am I right?'

Josh's belly twisted with frustration and he gripped the bars tighter. 'Does it matter? Melissa Gatner watched them kill a man, as well as a girl she lived with. She'll testify.'

'That will come out at trial, Mr Dellin.'

Josh let out a scoffing laugh. 'I got a notion a fair trial isn't too goddamn likely in this town.'

The marshal remained silent a moment and his shoulders sagged. 'I'll do the best I can to see that it is fair.'

'You know well as I do Miguel'll have whoever conducts the trial in his pocket. 'Less you're gonna handpick folks who aren't afraid to go against Chulo face to face, and in this town I'm bettin' that ain't even a number of one.'

The marshal swung in his chair, peered at Josh. 'Sayin' you're right, my hands are tied. I know damn well half the town saw what Brint and Billy did to you when you rode in, and in any other town maybe that would be enough to raise some sympathy. Reckon it did here as well. But it don't matter because even if by some act of God you managed to prove self-defense and walk free, you could not touch any of the Chulos legally and you know it. So that leaves you with killing them. And killing the sons of a man as connected and powerful as Miguel Chulo . . . you can see where I'm goin' with this, can't you?'

'Nothing I haven't thought myself a hundred times, Marshal, but another notion makes me figure it's worth the risk.'

'And what would that be, Mr Dellin?'

'The notion of how many women have ended up like that girl over to the funeral man's, and of how many more are going to wind up just like her by the time those boys are finished.'

The marshal's face darkened with the knowledge that everything Josh was telling him was true, and it had gone through his own mind. 'I saw her,' he said, voice low, strained. 'I went to the funeral man's and I saw her.'

'Right pretty sight, wasn't it, Marshal?' He didn't bother to conceal the sarcasm in his voice.

'I'll see it in my nightmares, damn sure.'

'Reckon you'll have company.'

'Those boys . . . hard to believe even they would do something so — ' He shuddered.

'Not when you look into their eyes, Marshal. Not hard to believe at all. Prairie wolves. Coyotes. Predators who hunt down their prey and tear it to pieces, sometimes for the sheer thrill of watching it die.'

'Mr Dellin . . . don't know what good this conversation is doing either of us, truly I don't. Seems like just a way to dwell on facts that can't be changed and to tear up one's innards over 'em.'

'Miguel, you see his face when he confronted me?'

The marshal's eyebrow cocked. 'What?'

'His face, his eyes. You look at them closely?'

'Did my best not to. Frankly, I don't need the reflection of my own cowardice staring back at me.'

'I did. I looked right into them. He's mean, like Marcus, and I got the notion he didn't give a damn about Brint being dead. He was more concerned with the slight against himself, a slight I caused because I defied him and everybody in town was going to know it unless he had you bring me in to make a public spectacle of my trial and hanging. Otherwise he would have let

Marcus just kill me.'

'Way I heard it, he was goddamned rough on those kids once his wife died. Never wanted young 'uns to begin with but once he had them he made sure they were protected from everybody but him. Probably ain't much of a surprise they grew up the way they did.'

'Reckon that might give you an out, Marshal.' Josh stared at the man, keeping his gaze and voice steady. He saw guilt in the lawdog's eyes, guilt and fear and indecision. Barsten struggled with his conscience and Josh intended to take full advantage of that.

'What the devil are you gettin' at, Dellin? Don't see an out anywhere. If there were I might have taken it by now.'

'You're a decent man, Marshal. Least you were once. I can see it. You got that dead girl on your mind and it's eating away at your soul.'

'I got a lot of goddamned things on my mind, Mr Dellin. And most of 'em are eatin' at my soul.'

'You're letting others make your choices. Same way that young woman with me let the men in Thanody make choices for her for too long. She decided to make her own when she came with me after those killers.'

The marshal laughed without humor. 'I don't have that option, Mr Dellin. Not no more.'

'Don't you? If Miguel cares more about his control than his sons, it won't much matter whether I kill one or three.'

The marshal's eyes widened and shock tightened his features. 'Are you plumb loco? You expect me just to let you go kill the other two. Miguel would hang me along with you.'

Josh's gaze held the marshal's. 'You want more dead women on your conscience? Justice won't get done unless you let me serve it.'

'You ain't talkin' about justice, you're talkin' about murder.'

'I'm talking about you letting me escape to take care of both those killers.

I'll turn myself in after and you can bring me to trial.'

'You must have taken a goddamn worse hit on the head from Brint than I figured if you think I'd go for that.'

'I think you'll go for that because of that young woman you saw to the hotel earlier. She'll be dead by morning if you don't. Marcus or Billy will come back and you won't be able to stop them from murdering her. Miguel threatened her and he'll have them follow through with it. You don't want her death on your mind, way that other girl's is. You're a good man, I figure. Good enough to see the truth.'

The marshal turned in his seat, showing his back to Josh, then thudded his boot-heels up on to the desk and set his cup on the blotter. He remained silent a moment, then in a low voice, said, 'I used to be a good man once, Mr Dellin. I used to have a notion right was right and that was all that mattered.'

Josh took a deep breath. 'I got a friend who felt the same way. We used to ride together till he accepted the law as absolute. But he's the one who sent me after these boys, for killing his sister-in-law. He changed, accepted some different truths. Way you could.'

'The truth I accepted was that right ain't always the easiest trail to follow and sometimes being right just don't matter in this world. Strength, power, fear . . . those things overrule it.'

'I ain't afraid of them, Marshal.'

'I . . . am, Mr Dellin. God help me, I am. I've done too many things I ain't proud of.'

'You got a chance to wipe that slate clean. I'm giving it to you.'

'You're wrong there, Mr Dellin. Because even if I was to do what you ask, the slate might be clean but my soul ain't ever likely to be. Those women these boys might have killed? I told myself they were somebody else's problem, somebody else's guilt, but I was wrong about that, too. Been wrong about too goddamned much in my life.'

'Then don't be wrong about letting

me protect that young woman at the hotel and putting an end to those boys' killing sprees.'

'What you're askin' me to do is just too much, Mr Dellin. Just too much.' The marshal went silent, took a sip from his coffee and Josh's belly knotted. He had seen something in the man, thought he had seen something, but he had come up short and now Melissa would die, soon, likely by morning. Chulo would move on her fast, because even if he bought off some of the council members or trial officials, he couldn't take a chance on a witness ruining anything.

Josh slumped, pressing his forehead against a bar and letting his eyes drift closed. Nothing in his life had ever meant much to him other than his career and his convictions, but now the one thing that suddenly meant everything was about to be taken from him. Fate had a way of mocking men like him, he reckoned. Making them its joke.

A sound interrupted his thoughts, the sound of a foot scuffing against the floor. He opened his eyes to see the marshal standing in front of the keys hanging on the wall peg, staring at them.

'Miguel Chulo's not goddamn stupid, Mr Dellin. Don't think he'd fall for the escape unless you leave a right big bruise. He would believe I was an idiot, already thinks that.'

The marshal reached for the keys, grabbed them, closing his fingers about them as if it were all he could do to hold on to them. He hesitated, then came over to the cell and unlocked the door.

Josh stepped out and the marshal drew his gun, offered it butt-first to Josh. 'Hit me in the jaw with the sidegate. Make sure you do it hard enough to leave a substantial welt.'

Josh nodded. 'Reckon you just made the smartest decision in a long spell, Marshal.'

The marshal offered a thin smile. 'Or the stupidest one.'

Josh hit him, then. The clack the gun made against his jaw sounded like a gunshot. The marshal staggered and went to his knees. Josh set the gun on the floor, then went to the desk, located his own gunbelt in the drawer and strapped it on.

He went to the door, paused, looked back at the law man, who held his hand to his jaw. 'You made the right choice, Marshal. You keep making them and that slate *will* be wiped clean.'

The marshal glanced over at him, eyes watery. 'You just make sure those boys don't kill any more women . . .'

'I aim to . . .'

★   ★   ★

With the setting sun bathing him in blood-red light Marcus Chulo circled back into Coyote Creek. His goddamn younger brother was off at the Wooden Pony Saloon doing whatever the hell he did behind its doors — Marcus damn well suspected but had no desire to witness such depravity by going to look for Billy there. Even *he* had his limits when it came to sin. Brint, the stupid sonofabitch, lay in a pine box over at the funeral man's and his father sat in his drawing room, coddling a brandy and a goddamn vicious attitude that Marcus had no desire to be on the other end of right now. He was, in fact, damn thankful the elder Chulo had instructed him to make certain that Thanotite woman never testified, even at a mock trial. He'd best take his time seeing to her fate, too. He'd let Billy return to the house first, because by the time Miguel Chulo put down a few brandies his wrath would turn toward the most convenient son, way it always did and always had. Marcus was too goddamn well familiar with the old man's pattern. A pattern that had forged his sons into the men they had become, prairie wolves that stalked their prey and took what they wanted.

'We are the hell you made us,' he whispered, slowing his horse as the sun dipped further into the distant mountains and shadows engulfed him. 'But I gotta admit, I goddamn like it.'

His blood surged with the thought of killing that woman. He wasn't much for fat ones but he'd make an exception before she died. Hell, he'd take his time all right, make sure she begged for her life and terror filled her eyes. Then he'd hurt her some more before actually finishing her off.

A grim smile pulled at his lips. After that maybe he'd mosey on over to the marshal's and make sure that manhunter didn't get a chance to stand trial. His father wanted Dellin made an example of in front of the town but he had let him walk away earlier today and now Brint was dead. Miguel didn't give a goddamn about one dead son, probably wouldn't had it been all three, but Marcus did. Brint was the brother to whom he'd been closest. Billy was like an idiot maverick, given to peculiar tastes; it should have been him who got his ticket punched. The marshal wouldn't stop Marcus this time and if he tried he might just as damn well join Dellin's funeral. No one in this town would dare try to bring charges against a Chulo for avenging a brother's death.

A shiver of uneasiness went through him at the thought that his father wouldn't be goddamn happy about it. The old man didn't like things on his doorstep, but this time Marcus was willing to risk it. If that manhunter somehow escaped it'd be Marcus's ass in a pine box and he wasn't goddamn fond of the notion.

Marcus angled his horse into an alley and dismounted, tethered the reins to a post beside the building. Only one goddamn fool in this town'd be stupid enough to rent a room to Dellin and his sow: Bittner. But he needed to determine in which room that girl was staying. He wagered that wouldn't be much of a problem.

He strolled around the corner, not bothering with even a pretense of stealth. Who would question him or stop him in this town? No one who wanted to go on breathing.

As he entered the hotel, he spotted nobody in the lobby or at the front desk, but a light seeped from the back room and he smiled.

He went to the room, stopping in the doorway to see Bittner sitting at a small desk, hunched over a ledger. The man must have sensed him, because he turned, and a startled look jumped on to his face.

'Surprised to see me, Bittner?' Marcus said. 'You shouldn't be. Harboring enemies of the Chulos is a speciality of yours, ain't it? Couldn't be you're still holdin' a grudge 'cause my father took your land?'

'What do you want, Marcus?' the man asked, trying to keep his composure but fear made his voice shake.

'Which room is that girl in, the Thanotite woman?'

'I-I don't know what you're talkin' about.'

Marcus drew his Smith & Wesson,

aimed it at the man. 'You know better than to give me such a damn fool answer.'

Bittner's face washed pale and his shoulders slumped. 'Room 6.'

'Much obliged.' Marcus smiled, reached back and closed the door to the small room.

'What . . . what are you doing?' the little hotel man asked, panic lighting in his eyes. He stood, backed against the desk.

Marcus walked up to him jammed the gun barrel deep into the man's belly and pulled the trigger.

The hotel man's body muffled the shot somewhat, but Marcus didn't give a damn who heard it.

Marcus withdrew the gun and the clerk's eyelids fluttered. He pitched forward, slammed into the floor face-first.

'Never did cotton much to traitors,' Marcus whispered as he knelt and wiped the blood on his gunbarrel on the man's shirt, then holstered the weapon. Standing, he went to the door, opened it and peered out into the lobby, seeing no one.

With a low laugh, he took the stairs at a slow pace, expectation and eagerness making his armpits sweat and his heart pound. Killing the hotel man had only been a prelude, but the copper scent of blood in his nostrils and sight of death in his memory sent a murder fever raging through his veins. How he enjoyed that feeling, lusted after it. For an instant his surroundings vanished and only a drumming rhythm — kill, kill, kill — filled his brain. Then flashes of times when his father's fists had pummeled him into submission, explosions of black rage in the old man's eyes that obliterated any compassion a father might have ever felt for a son. Replaced by glimpses of the faces of men and women Marcus had killed, swirling before him, terror-stricken, pleading, agonized —

He uttered an unbidden laugh and suddenly he was back in the hallway, the sound of his voice echoing around him. He shuddered, eyes narrowing, breathing suddenly labored.

'Jesus,' he muttered, blood-fever still trembling through his soul.

A single wall lantern, turned low, lit the hallway. Buttery light shined from red-foil wallpaper and the threadbare carpet muffled his footsteps.

Licking his lips, he reached the room, knocked lightly. A voice came from within and he smiled. 'Gave me the right room, Bittner. Thank you kindly.'

'Who is it?'

Marcus' dark eyes glittered, expectation growing. Blood butterflies fluttered in his belly. 'Marshal, ma'am,' he said, doubting it would work.

No sound came from within for a moment, then came the thud of footsteps going away from the door.

'Damn whore's smarter than she looked,' he mumbled and snapped out a foot. His boot-heel slammed into the door above the lock and the door bounded inward.

He caught the door edge on the

rebound and stepped inside. The girl was at the window, trying to raise it. He darted across the room, grabbed her, then hurled her around and threw her on to the bed. She came up instantly, tried to run. He caught her again, jabbed a fist into her face. She collapsed to her knees, fingers going to her bleeding lips.

Marcus stared at her, then went to the door and closed it. The latch ruined, the door drifted back open a crack.

'You won't be testifyin' to nothin', you fat cow,' Marcus said, grinning. 'You shoulda stayed in Thanody, way we told ya to.'

Terror flooded Melissa's eyes and she tried to scramble back on hands and knees.

Marcus stooped, grabbed her dress and hauled her up on to the bed, then came down on top of her. 'I'm surely gonna kill you, you dumb cow, but first we're gonna have ourselves some fun. I'm figurin' on you bein' a right soft ride . . .'

10

Josh made his way from the marshal's office to the hotel, keeping to the shadows and avoiding contact with any of the townsfolk. He had no idea who to trust and any one of them might take word of his escape back to Miguel Chulo before he wanted it discovered. After he got Melissa safely out of town — though persuading her to go was still problematic — he would see to the two remaining Chulo boys. Billy would be first. He would be the easier, though Josh still needed to find out which saloon a man of Billy's tastes would frequent. He hoped the hotel man might know that.

Marcus would be harder to catch off guard, but sooner or later he would come looking for his younger sibling and Josh would be waiting for him.

What about Miguel Chulo? The man

had threatened Melissa and as long as he remained free that threat would hang over her head, even without his sons. Chulo was a powerful man, with the means to pay a hired killer to finish the job he would not dirty his own hands with. But proving something against him, with his connections . . . Josh saw damn little chance of that. And hanging him . . . that would likely put a price on Josh's own head, if killing the sons didn't.

Fact was, at this juncture, he didn't quite know what to do about the man, but he would worry about that after he finished with the boys.

He paused across the street from the hotel, waiting for some passers-by to make it a few hundred feet down the boardwalk before he chanced crossing. With the falling night the street was lit by hanging lanterns but enough shadow remained to make it necessary for him to cross a lighted patch only briefly. Using caution, he slipped into the lobby, but saw nobody around. He noticed the door behind the counter slightly ajar, a light showing from within. He went toward it, intending to question the hotel man about Billy Chulo's habits before he went up to Melissa's room, but ten feet from the door he paused, a dark feeling washing over him. Nothing he could put a finger on, but his manhunter's sixth sense had kicked in and his hand drifted to the butt of his Peacemaker. He eased forward, coming up to the right of the door.

'Bittner?' he said. Only the sound of his quickening heart beat answered.

Josh pressed the flat of his hand against the panel and sent the door swinging inward. When no sound or shots came he peered around the corner and dread made his belly plunge.

'Christ!' He stepped into the room, which was empty except for the body lying on its stomach on the floor.

He went to the corpse, knelt and turned it over. A hole gaped in the hotel man's belly. He didn't need a crystal ball to tell him the Chulos were behind the killing and why.

He straightened, backed quickly from the room and ran for the stairs, his dread strengthening. Whichever Chulo had murdered the hotel man would have a second target on his list: Melissa.

Josh took the stairs in bounds, using much less caution than he should have. Emotion overrode his normal prudence. He bolted down the hallway, hand clamped to the butt of his Peacemaker.

Melissa's door was ajar and at a glance he saw splintered wood about the latch, telling him it had been forced.

He drew up, listened, his heart pounding, his breath beating out. A woman's voice came from within, then a man's, laced with obscenities.

Josh kicked the door open, ready to draw his gun. The sight that met him sent fury surging through his veins. Marcus Chulo straddled Melissa, who lay half-on, half-off the bed. Chulo's head swiveled as Josh froze, and a curse came from his lips.

'Goddammit, Dellin, I was just getting started. How the hell'd you get out of jail?'

Josh didn't waste time answering. He couldn't shoot the outlaw without the risk of hitting Melissa, so he bolted across the room, and flung himself at Marcus Chulo.

The killer disentangled himself from the young woman and came up, twisting, just as Josh grabbed his shirt. Josh hurled Marcus sideways, away from Melissa.

'You all right?' he asked, not taking his gaze from Marcus, who stumbled sideways.

'Yes,' she said, pushing herself up.

Josh spun, lunged at Chulo again, swinging an uppercut that came nearly from the floor. Marcus cranked his head sideways but still took enough of the blow to send him staggering a few steps backward.

Josh threw a straight right, nailing the

outlaw flush in the nose, and blood spurted across his knuckles.

Marcus let out a roar and swung a left hook. Josh ducked, came up with another uppercut. Bone hit chin and Marcus's teeth slammed together. Blood sprayed from his mouth. A glaze washed across his eyes, but only for an instant. The brother recovered faster than Josh expected, launched an awkward kick that raked Josh's shin. Pain spiked through his lower leg but he barely noticed it. He couldn't recollect ever having been driven by such blind rage and it all came from the thought of anything happening to that innocent young woman standing near the bed.

'Goddammit, Dellin!' yelled Marcus, suddenly grabbing Josh's shirt and jerking him close. 'I told my father we should have just killed you outright.' He slammed his forehead into Josh's face. Stars exploded before the manhunter's eyes. For a second, blackness threatened the edges of his mind but he shook his head, regaining his composure.

Josh jerked up a knee, burying it in Chulo's crotch. He couldn't take any chances with the man. He needed to get enough room to draw and put an end to the fight before Marcus, who appeared to be built out of bull, managed to kill him and the young woman.

Marcus blew out a spray of blood-flecked spittle and doubled, clutching his southern parts. Josh snapped a right cross, cracking the man flush in the temple, then brought his knee up again, slamming it into Marcus's gaping mouth.

The blow straightened Marcus bolt upright. He staggered backward, gasping.

Any other man would have gone down at that point, but Marcus Chulo remained on his feet, wobbly, but still dangerous enough to go for his gun.

Josh's hand slapped for his Peacemaker. The gun came up in a blur, but Marcus's draw was damn near as fast.

Josh twisted as he drew, triggered the

three remaining shots in his gun; he hadn't reloaded since downing Brint Chulo.

Marcus's gun blasted a beat behind, but in his case speed overrode aim. The bullet buried itself in a wall, missing Josh only by fractions.

Two of Josh's shots hit home, punching into Marcus Chulo's chest and kicking him backward. A look of shock crashed on to the man's olive features. He kept going, straight into the window and on through. Glass exploded and his body seemed suddenly to suspend in midair, before dropping. Josh, despite the ringing gun blasts throbbing in his ears, heard the body crash into a wooden awning below the window, then thud on to the ground.

Heart pounding, he holstered his gun and went to the young woman, drawing her into his arms. She clutched him like a drowning swimmer grabbing a passing log. Tears soaked through his shirt and sobs wracked her body.

'Shhh, it's all right. We got two of them. Just one left to go.'

'So much violence,' she whispered, a sob punctuating her words. 'And I couldn't move . . . I couldn't help . . . '

'It doesn't matter. All that matters is we get you out of here now, before Miguel sends his last son or hires someone else to do his dirty work.'

She pulled back, shaking her head, tears streaking down her face. 'I'm not leaving you, I told that. That goes for now more than ever.'

Josh shook his head, frowned. 'Dammit, Melissa, you have to. I have to get the last of them.'

'And what about Miguel? He'll never give up, even if you kill Billy, and you know it. He'll send someone after me, after us.'

Josh nodded. 'I know, but I'll figure that out after I get Billy.'

'I'm not leaving.' Determination set in her tone and he knew there would be no arguing with her.

'Reckon maybe I shouldn't have

encouraged you about makin' up your own mind till this was over.' He gave her a wink, trying to lighten the dread crawling through his belly.

She laughed, a soft sweet sound, but also one laced with nervousness. 'That's what you get for sowing independence, Mr Dellin.'

He glanced at the broken window. 'The marshal will be here soon. He let me escape, but if I'm here when he comes he'll be forced to take me in again. Miguel will see to that.' He reached into his pocket, pulled out a key. 'Go to my room and lock the door. Keep quiet until I knock twice, then knock twice again. Don't let anyone else in or make a sound if someone should come.'

She nodded and took the key. He eased into the hallway, then went down to the lobby. After locating a back door, he slipped out into the night.

Two hours must have gone by and Josh Dellin felt every single second of each. Voices came from the crowd that had gathered in the street and the sound of the marshal questioning anybody as to whether they had witnessed what occurred drifted to his ears. One man answered he had seen Marcus Chulo crash through the window but hadn't seen anything further. The second brother was dead, either by Josh's bullets or by the fall, of that he was certain. Josh saw a wagon cross in front of the alley, Marcus' booted feet hanging off the back.

Two down. One to go. And no sign of the elder Chulo, though for certain somebody would have informed him of his son's death by now.

Another half hour trickled by. Josh, nestled behind a crate, sighed, ants crawling through his nerves. He was sick of this damn waiting, but didn't dare move until the crowd dispersed.

It took another fifteen minutes before they drifted off and silence settled in the street. He eased out from behind the crate and stood in the darkness of the alley.

A man was poised at the alley entrance, peering in. As he took a step forward, Josh's hand eased to his gun, though he reckoned it wouldn't do him a lick of good since he hadn't reloaded.

'Reckoned you'd be hanging around waitin' on the crowd to go,' came the marshal's voice. 'Also reckon I don't have to ask if you're responsible for Marcus meetin' his maker.'

'When I got to the hotel he was already in the room, trying to rape Melissa.'

The lawdog nodded. 'Got his just, then. Where's the girl?'

'Had her lock herself in my hotel room till I come for her. I s'pect you found the hotel man?'

'Found him. Marcus responsible for that?'

Josh nodded. 'One more to go, Marshal.'

'Billy.'

'You got a notion where a man of his tastes might pass the time?'

'I've seen him come and go drunk

from the Wooden Pony. Hear tell some mighty strange things go on there. Don't even know if his brothers know he sneaks off there.'

'Likely they know but don't care to confirm it.'

'You could be right.'

Josh drew his gun, reloaded from bullets in his belt. 'All works out, you might be able to go back to being a real lawman.'

'Not as long as Miguel runs the territory.'

'Aim to do something about that, too, just don't know what yet. Sure bet he's not going to take the loss of his sons lying down. He might not give a damn they're dead, but he gives a damn about his hold on this town.'

Josh brushed past the marshal, paused at the alley entrance, peering into the street.

'Down the street to the right, near the outskirts of town.'

Josh looked back, nodded. 'Obliged, Marshal.'

'Don't thank me for risking your life instead of mine. If I weren't such a coward I might have done something about them before they . . . well, before that woman ended up at the funeral man's.'

'You know what they say about hindsight.' Josh slipped from the alley and kept to the shadows as he made his way towards the Wooden Pony Saloon. While he couldn't be certain Billy would be there with all that had happened, he preferred to check the saloon before riding out to the Chulo homestead.

The usual amount of swearing, whore laughter and piano-clinking was absent from the Wooden Pony. The place seemed almost serene compared to any other saloon he'd visited and only the buttery glow bleeding through the large front window and batwings indicated it was even in business. Josh edged up to the window, peered through and scanned the small room for any signs of Billy Chulo. What he saw gave him pause — it was the opposite extreme to Thanody, he reckoned, a place catering to men and women of different tastes. He couldn't recollect ever having seen the likes, though he'd heard tell of such places.

Of Billy Chulo he saw no sign, so he eased away from the window and drifted around the corner to the side of the building. Darkness became intense and he could barely pick out the outline of an outside stairway. He hesitated, not certain he wanted to go up and take a closer look at what was going on behind closed doors, but if Billy was up there he had little choice. Waiting around all night for the outlaw to wander out wasn't an option.

He crept forward and from atop the stairway a figure rose from a sitting position. Josh hadn't seen it in the darkness until there was movement.

Josh's hand went to the butt of his Peacemaker as the man clomped down the steps, obviously somewhat drunk.

'Hear tell you relieved me of both my

brothers, Mr Dellin. Shame that now I'm going to have to kill such a handsome man such as yourself.'

Josh recognized the voice. 'I aim to arrest you, Billy Chulo, for the murder of that young woman from Thanody and countless others untold.'

The youngest brother stood three steps above Josh, now. 'Do ya now? What makes you think you can just do that, since I was here waitin' on you?'

The truth dawned on Josh with a crash. Billy *had* been waiting. And that meant —

Something slammed into the back of Josh's head and he went down, the dark world swirling before his vision. Pain radiated through his skull and he felt a hand at his waist, relieving him of his gun. He pushed up to his hands and knees, struggling to focus.

'Come now, Mr Dellin,' a voice came from behind him. 'You honestly think I didn't know of my son's peculiar tastes? I know everything that goes on in this town. Didn't figure it would be long before you sought to murder the last of my offspring, though I will admit it came faster than I expected.'

The voice . . . Miguel Chulo's. They'd set him up, expected him. Most outlaws weren't smart enough but he'd forgotten he was dealing with a man who controlled a town.

He didn't get long to think on it because a boot crashed into his head and Billy Chulo's laughter rang behind it. Josh hit the ground on his face. Billy grabbed him under the arms and flipped him over while Miguel slipped a lasso around his torso.

'Go to the hotel and find the girl,' Miguel Chulo ordered Billy. 'Then come back here. We're going to give Mr Dellin what he intended giving you. We'll show this town what happens to anyone stupid enough to defy the Chulos.'

Billy hurried from the alley.

Miguel leaned over Josh, peering down. Josh could barely see the outline of his face in the darkness. 'I think your woman will enjoy watching you die before we kill her, too, don't you, Mr Dellin?'

Josh didn't get the chance to respond. A boot-heel crashed into his temple and the world suddenly got a whole lot darker.

11

Consciousness trickled back, accompanied by a throbbing in his face and skull. A blurry patch of light focused into a hanging lantern and Josh realized he was on his back, staring up. With a thundering in his head, he twisted to discover he lay in the main street of Coyote Creek, his hands tied in front of him, stretched above his head and secured to the saddle of a horse.

He blinked, focusing on the man sitting in the saddle — Miguel Chulo. Beside the senior Chulo, atop another horse, sat Billy, peering down at him, a grin on his face, eyes glazed.

'You find the girl?' Miguel asked, not looking at his son, but keeping his gaze on Josh.

Billy shook his head. 'She wasn't in the room.' His words came slightly slurred.

'We'll find her later.' Miguel said. 'I warned you, Mr Dellin. I told you to leave things alone. Now we'll make an example of you to make certain no one else in this town gets any ideas about questioning my rule.' He twisted his head, gazed at his son. 'Find the marshal. I want to talk to him.'

Billy nodded, slid down from his horse and went toward the marshal's office. He returned a short time later, the lawdog in tow. Barsten's bruised face carried a defeated look.

'You let him escape, Barsten?' Miguel's gaze probed the lawdog's, apparently seeing the answer he suspected, that Barsten had purposely let Josh go. 'I will deal with you later on that point. For now I'm telling you we are going to see to it a killer receives justice.' Miguel patted a coiled noose secured to his saddle. Billy climbed back atop his horse.

'You can't do this.' Barsten frowned, shifted feet, body tense, hesitant. 'He ain't had a trial.'

'He murdered two of my sons.'

Miguel flicked a glance at Josh, then back to the marshal. 'I see no need for a trial. You have any other ideas we won't have need of a marshal, either.'

Barsten's lips pressed together and crimson welled in his cheeks. But he didn't move. He glanced at Josh. 'I'm sorry,' he whispered, head lowering, gaze locking on the boardwalk.

Josh could see townsfolk had gathered along the boardwalks, their faces somber, as if their last chance of freedom were slipping away yet they were still too paralyzed with fear or complacency to do anything about it.

Miguel's gaze swept over them. 'Let this be a lesson to you all. This man is a killer and this is what happens to killers in my town — *yah*!'

Miguel's heels slapped into the sides of his chestnut and the animal bolted. The line jerked tight and Josh suddenly felt as if his arms had been wrenched out of their sockets. Gravel and hard ground tore at him as he was dragged through the street. Out of instinct, he gripped the rope leading from his wrists with both hands but it did no good. His body bounced along as if it were a sack of flour, every jounce causing pain. Fabric tore from his shirt and blood welled from skinned patches on his chest. Dust and dirt choked his nostrils and clogged his mouth. The thunder of the horses' hoofs drummed in his ears and Billy's laugh punctuated the roar.

A moment later the horse slowed and he came to a stop, groaning, bleeding, half-conscious. Blood and dust soured his mouth and pain sang from every muscle and joint.

Miguel slipped from his mount, Billy following suit. They came over to him, untied the rope leading to the animal. Each man grabbed an arm, then hauled him up and dragged him to Billy's horse.

Miguel stepped back, grabbed the coiled rope from his saddle, the end of which was knotted into a noose. He slung it over a branch of the cottonwood they'd stopped before.

Josh could barely stand. He leaned heavily against the horse.

Miguel cast Billy a look, then the remaining Chulo brother grabbed Josh's arm and spun him to face the horse.

'Up into the saddle, Dellin,' Billy ordered.

Josh jammed a foot into the stirrup and Billy hoisted him up the rest of the way. Josh got both hands, wrists still tied, about the horn.

Billy led the horse beneath the rope hanging from the branch.

Miguel Chulo looked up at him, expression smug. 'I normally don't resort to taking care of such matters myself, Mr Dellin, but you've left me no choice. I do not give a damn that my sons are gone. They were crude worthless boys and, frankly, I was weary of cleaning up their messes. But I do care about my reputation and I will not tolerate any damage to it. This town is mine and will remain so. And I am certain the governor will see it as a favor, ridding the West of a man of your sort.'

Josh glanced at Billy. 'That concern

you at all, son? Your father not giving a damn about what happened to your kin or to you?'

Billy grinned, his laudanum-glazed eyes watery. 'Doesn't concern me a bit, Dellin. I figgered it out a long time ago.' The youngest son cast a look at his father Josh couldn't read entirely, one that might have said Billy Chulo had plans to repay his father someday, but now would not be the time. With that look, Josh's slim hope of turning the son against his father vanished.

'Any last words, Mr Dellin?' asked Miguel, the smug expression growing stronger.

'The term rot in hell comes to mind,' Josh said.

Miguel uttered a laugh laced with contempt. 'Put the rope around his neck . . . '

★ ★ ★

Sounds came from next door, in Melissa's former room. Someone stomping around, muttering to himself. She huddled in the darkness of Josh's hotel room, sitting on the edge of the bed. Arms wrapped about herself, she listened, heart pounding in her throat. Whoever it was, he was making no pretense of stealth. It could not be Josh, so that left one likely possibility, the remaining Chulo brother, Billy.

She waited, holding her breath until the noises stopped. Footsteps clomped in the hallway but they didn't stop before Josh's door.

She let out her breath and shuddered, unable to calm her racing heart.

Violence. She had seen so much in the past day and it repulsed her. Perhaps if the men of Thanody were right in anything, it was that violence was a corrosive thing, something that fed on itself, something to be avoided.

But, perhaps, sometimes people had no alternative, when life and liberty were threatened and there was no choice but to defend what was theirs, or what was right. To keep something precious. And as much as violence repulsed her, it was also a reality of the world in which she lived. Perhaps some day it would not be, but for now . . .

Noises came from the street, muffled. She stood, then went to the window and lifted it. She peered at the street below, her heart stopping, then suddenly starting again with a harsh thundering as fear swelled in her veins. Townsfolk had gathered in the middle of the street. A man lay in the dirt, hands tied to a line leading to a horse. A moment later, the marshal came out on to the boardwalk with Billy Chulo, whom she was certain had been searching for her in her room a few minutes previous.

'No!' she gasped, hands going to her mouth. Josh. It was Josh tied to that horse. Something had gone wrong. Her gaze went to the older man on the horse, whom she reckoned could only be Miguel Chulo. It was clear what they intended to do.

She backed from the window, shaking, fighting the waves of panic washing through her. They were going to kill him; she had no doubt of that. And she had no weapon, no way of stopping them, and even if Josh had left her a gun she had no idea how to use one and firing it at another human being . . .

She ran to the door, ignoring the panic and indecision. If they killed Josh she saw no point in hiding herself, living in fear.

She ran down the hall, then stumbled down the stairs and across the lobby. Bursting out on to the boardwalk, she heard the elder Chulo let out a *yah!* that sent his horse careening through the street. She screamed, one of the few times she'd ever given in to such a show of emotion. She'd never been allowed to express such things in Thanody, but that no longer mattered, did it?

She ran across the street, toward the marshal, who looked at her with defeat and sadness as she came up to him.

'You have to stop them!' she yelled, grabbing his arm.

'Ma'am, I can't. Your fella got himself into it — '

'Coward!' she screamed, every ounce of repressed emotion she carried over the years surging, geysering out. 'You can't just let them kill him. If you do your town will never have a chance.'

'I *gave* your fella a chance. There's nothing I can do.' The marshal turned and started to walk away.

'No! Don't let him die, Marshal. There's only two of them.'

He looked back at her. 'And one of me, 'less you plan on helpin'.'

Tears flowed from her eyes. 'Those men will keep on killing and you'll forever be under Miguel Chulo's thumb. Is that what you want? I lived that way all my life, Marshal. I let men more powerful than me tell me how to dress and how to talk and what to do each day of my life and the only thing it got me was murdered friends and no self-respect. I'll do anything to save him. I won't be a coward any more.'

He peered at her, shame coming into his eyes, shook his head, then went back into his office.

She turned, started down the board-walk, having no idea what she could do to stop those men from killing Josh but knowing she had no choice but to try.

'Wait!' a voice came from behind her and she looked back to see the marshal coming out of his office again, a rifle in his hand. He levered a shell into the chamber.

'Just point and pull the trigger.'

'I-I can't — ' she stammered, as he thrust the rifle into her hands.

'What was that speech you just gave me about doing anything to save your fella? I ain't riskin' my hide 'less you back me up and that means you might have to kill a man. And while we're standing here jawin' about it time's runnin' out.'

She grabbed the rifle and spun, ran. The marshal clomped along behind her.

The horses had stopped just beyond town and she headed right for them, gasping for air, sweat pouring from her face and running from beneath her arms. Her heart pounded and panicked thoughts cascaded through her mind. She had told the marshal she would do anything to save Josh but when it came down to pulling the trigger, killing another man . . .

The thought nearly made her stumble, fall.

She had no choice, she told herself. If she froze this time, Josh would die.

★   ★   ★

Josh straightened in the saddle as Billy reached up for the noose. His gaze focused straight ahead and he suddenly noticed figures running toward them from town.

'Christ, no,' he whispered, his belly sinking. Dammit, he'd told her to hide . . .

Miguel Chulo heard the commotion and spun.

Billy's hand withdrew and his gaze swung towards the runners as well. 'I'll be damned, the marshal grew a pair — ' His hand swept toward the gun at his hip.

The marshal spotted the move, tried to pull his own Peacemaker. He was too late. Billy feathered the trigger and a gory rose bloomed on the lawdog's chest. Barsten jumped backwards in mid-stride, slammed into the ground on his back and lay still.

Josh kicked Billy in the side of the head an instant after he pulled the trigger. The gun flew from the man's hand and he staggered.

Gripping the horn, Josh swung his body from the saddle, landing on his feet. He threw another kick at Billy, slamming a boot-heel into the man's knee. Billy's leg buckled and he collapsed, clutching at it and letting out a shriek.

Miguel Chulo whirled, grabbed the Peacemaker from his belt he'd taken from Josh and swung it toward the manhunter.

After casting a quick backward look at Melissa, who had stopped and was shaking as she gripped the rifle, Miguel adjusted his aim on Josh and laughed. 'Thanotites — ' he jeered, mockery in his tone. 'Adios, Mr Dellin.'

A shot blasted, echoing through the night. Josh tensed, expecting a bullet to punch through his chest.

But it did not. Miguel stiffened, the Peacemaker unfired. The gun dropped from his fingers and he collapsed to his knees. He gave Josh a last vicious look before falling on to his face.

Behind him stood Melissa, the rifle barrel smoking, her hands bone-white as she clutched it. Her face had washed pale and her lips quivered. She suddenly flung the rifle down as if she'd grabbed a branding iron, then fell to her knees, sobbing.

Josh struggled out of the ropes that bound his wrists, tossed them aside. Then he grabbed Billy and hoisted the screeching Chulo up into the saddle.

'Reckon you deserve no better than what you intended for me.' He placed the rope around Billy's neck and slapped the horse on the rump. The animal bolted, leaving Billy Chulo kicking at air and making gagging noises. Those noises ceased a few moments later.

Josh went to the woman, offered her a hand. She came to her feet, collapsed against his chest and he held her tight. 'Shhh, you did the only thing you could do. You saved my life . . . '

'I . . . he was going to kill you . . . I . . . '

'You made a choice, on your own this time. That's a hell of a lot harder than letting others make it for you . . . but you made the right one.'

He held her for long moments, while behind him the body of Billy Chulo swayed in the rising moonlight.

12

Two days had passed since the deaths of the Chulo brothers and their father. Josh had remained in Coyote Creek, explaining to the folks there they would have to make their own choices from now on and the first would be to hire a marshal they could trust never to allow the same situation they'd lived under for so long to prevail ever again. Barsten, in the final tally, had turned out to be a good man, but his weakness had contributed to what amounted to enslavement and needless deaths.

Still, the town would have some difficulty adjusting but he reckoned you could only set people up to make their own choices, not hold their hands through each. Freedom came with a price and soul-searching.

He and Melissa had hit the trail early this morning, ridden south. They had one other stop to make before heading back to tell Tredder his sister-in-law had been avenged and the men responsible were all dead.

'We don't have to do this,' he said, glancing at her.

She peered at him, her face weary, but brighter than it had been for two days. He reckoned she was coming to grips with things she'd long held as truths. He reckoned he had done the same thing.

This was his last case. A manhunter just knew when it was time to hang up his gun, and that time, for him, was now. He had other things on his mind, like a small ranch and maybe even a wife . . .

'I want to do it,' she said. 'I reckon I need to.'

They rode the rest of the way in silence until they reached Thanody. Townsfolk stared at them as they rode in, mostly at Melissa, who was wearing a riding skirt with buckshot sewn into the hem and a white blouse instead of the traditional Thanotite garb.

Josiah Herridge came out of the general store on to the boardwalk, his eyes dark with anger as he gazed up at her.

They reined up near the tree in the center of town, which still held the undergarments.

'What are you doing back in Thanody, Mr Dellin? And what is this blasphemy you are wearing, Melissa?'

The young woman ignored him, slid down from her saddle and went to the tree. She began plucking the undergarments from the branches, gathering them in her arms.

'What are you doing?' Herridge's face flushed with crimson as he stormed from the boardwalk into the street. 'I forbid you! Stop that this minute!'

Josh pinned the man with his gaze. 'She don't take orders from you, Mr Herridge. Not any more. That young woman those men took is dead. They killed her. I saw to it she got a proper burial. Then I let the buzzards have their fill of the men responsible.'

'They're dead?' Herridge said, something close to relief moving into his eyes.

'That doesn't avenge that poor girl but I reckon your Devil will see to that. Reckon your God will have words with you for allowing them to take her, too.'

He swung his gaze toward Melissa, who went to one of the women on the boardwalk and handed her the undergarments. She came back to her horse, climbed into the saddle.

They rode out of Thanody, Herridge staring after them. A small smile trickled on to Josh's lips. He suddenly felt comfortable, content, even, a feeling he reckoned he hadn't experienced since the early days in his former career. As if all the gray had bled from the world . . .

THE GUN HAND

Robert Anderson

Johnny Royal had lived on his wits and his gun after leaving home following a foolish argument. Returning home, however, he finds the neighbourhood is threatened by rustlers and outlaws. He meets a local rancher, the beautiful Sarah, whose uncle's past criminal deeds have returned to haunt them. Now, Johnny, Sarah and the ranch foreman must blaze a path of destruction against the forces searching for her uncle's ill-gotten gains, in the teeth of the outlaw's meanest gunslingers.

TOO MANY SUNDOWNS

Jake Douglas

Chance Benbow thought he had found the place — and the woman — which would bring him peace and quiet and a future. But then it all blew up in his face. When he recovered from the bullet wounds, he saw his future clearly, albeit clouded by gunsmoke. He would stride through it with a gun in each hand — and if hell waited on the other side, then he would meet it head-on, taking a lot of dead men with him.

GUN FOR REVENGE

Steve Hayes

While Gabriel Moonlight hides out in Mexico, Ellen Kincaide asks him to avenge the death of her sister and Gabriel's former girlfriend, Cally. He refuses, but when Ellen is kidnapped by bandits Gabriel sets out to rescue her. Then he has a change of heart and promises to kill the man who murdered Cally. But he discovers the identity of the murderer and knows that to exact retribution means almost certain death. Even so, a promise is a promise.